Magic & Mayhem

Magic &

Mayhem

4 Whitney & Davies Short Stories

By

E.L. Bates

*Including a bonus chapter of Glamours & Gunshots, the
next Whitney & Davies book!*

ISBN-10: 0-9899551-6-8
ISBN-13: 978-0-9899551-6-4

FIRST EDITION

Cover design by E.L. Bates

StarDance Press
stardancepress.com

The Third Thief: Maia Whitney has returned home for her sister's wedding determined to stay aloof from family dramas. Alas, the disappearance of a valuable and possibly cursed bracelet alters her plans. Can this magician's apprentice solve the crime and save her sister's wedding from doom and disaster?

Many Magical Returns: On Susannah's seventeenth birthday, she learns why her mother has always insisted she never use magic in front of Uncle Ernie. Escaping her uncle's greed and learning magic on the run are tall orders, but one thing is certain: this is a birthday Susannah will never forget.

Passion & Practicality: Steady, sensible Evelyn has always looked after and protected her flighty, feather-brained older sister Violet. So when Violet accidentally kills a man, of course Evelyn is going to take the blame. But her former fiancé Henry, now working for the magicians' Domestic Protection Agency, has other plans.

Masks & the Magician: Who is the mysterious woman? Is she the Grand Duchess Anastasia, as she claims, or a fraud? The English magician calling himself Merlin has his own ideas, but untangling truth from lie is a difficult task in this mission. When everyone wears a mask, who can be trusted?

The Third
Thief

Maia Whitney loved her family; however, not two minutes after entering the Whitney house the day before her sister's wedding she wished them at the bottom of the North Sea. It was a good reminder of why she had left home to live and work with her mother's sister, Aunt Amelia Rawlings.

She could have found a tutor closer to home, one who was perhaps less intractable. But underneath Maia's spoken desire to apprentice to one of England's greatest magicians had been the driving need to leave home and let her family go their way while she, at long last, went hers.

Aside from a few years in France during the war, Maia had always been the stay-at-home, stick-in-the-mud, dutiful, responsible, eldest daughter. The discovery last autumn of her magical abilities and subsequent apprenticeship to her aunt had changed that irrevocably.

Her family had yet to catch up on the changes.

"May! You're here at last, what kept you? Come sew up the hem of my wedding dress, I caught it on something when I put it on to show to Cousin Edith earlier and it tore!" wailed Ellie in one breathless rush from the bedroom.

Mrs. Whitney bustled into the front hall and scowled at Maia, who had not yet had a chance to remove her hat. "Mrs. Tate insists she told me we didn't have room for all the guests, but I am certain she said we *did*, and now here's your father's dearest, er, second or third cousins or something, with no place to sleep! The shame of it! Maia, you'll simply have to share a room with Merry, that's all there is to it, and kindly explain to Mrs. Tate that she must do a better job maintaining order if she wants to remain as housekeeper at Stanbury!"

"A housekeeper is a ridiculous affectation in this day and

age for a household of only three people, and you know it, Mama," Merry said heatedly, following her mother into the hall and nodding distractedly at her sister. The youngest of the three Whitney sisters had moderated her Socialist tendencies recently but had not done away with them entirely. "We really shouldn't be living in such a large establishment at all. Think of the better uses to which this house and land could be put!"

Mother and daughter began a lively debate over the responsibilities of the gentry to the land, their ancestral homes, and the lower classes. Ellie continued to wail unseen that her wedding was going to be ruined if her dress wasn't fixed *right then*, and various members of the extended Whitney and Rawlings families popped in and out to share their opinions on those and other matters.

Maia's head began to ache.

A year ago, she would have felt it her duty to help Ellie, calm her mother, talk some sense into Merry, beg Mrs. Tate not to leave them in a huff, and play hostess to her various uncles, aunts, and cousins.

Today, she raised her voice to be heard over the clamor.

"I told you in my last three letters, Mama, I'm staying with Julia and Dan at Little Oaks rather than add to the guest list here. Ellie, you know Susan Abbott in the village will mend your dress far better than I could—she is a seamstress, after all. I will see you all at the dinner tonight; I only stopped in to let you know I had arrived safely from London. Give my love to Father when he comes in."

Maia did not need to be told Mr. Whitney had escaped to the farthest edges of the estate and would return only when he had to prepare for the formal dinner that evening.

Maia made her own escape out the front door she had barely entered, her family's complaints and recriminations following her. Once, guilt would have made her turn back. Now, she could—

Not laugh, not quite yet. But she could at least smile wryly and leave with only the mildest sense of irritation.

Walking through the woods between Stanbury and Little Oaks brought a wave of memories. The last time she had been this way was in September, a moonlit evening whose beauty had been spoiled by a murder happening beneath her very nose.

That had been most unpleasant, but as Maia dawdled along the hedge-lined path this June morning with the birds singing overhead and the scent of wild roses filling her nose, a dreamy smile played about her lips.

The murder itself had been dreadful, of course, but it had led to her discovery of magic—real magic, not stage tricks or superstitious witchcraft. She had learned that unknown to most, some people possessed the ability to manipulate the natural world through magic. And she was one of them.

That night had also introduced her to Lennox Davies, a magician equally endearing and irritating, who worked for Magical Intelligence, the secret agency protecting the British Empire from magical threats.

She and Len had started out at odds with each other, but by the time they had solved the murder and saved England from magical disaster, they were fast friends. Maia had hoped to see Len at the wedding tomorrow, as he and the bridegroom were old friends, but he'd sent her a scrawled note a month ago saying he was still in Russia on a job and wouldn't return in time for the festivities.

Memories and discreet practice of a few basic spells occupied Maia all the way to the Foy estate.

Little Oaks was a stately old brick building, not as venerable as Stanbury but still distinguished, with creepers growing over the walls and its three stories dominating the surrounding landscape. At the moment, its peaceful repose in the summer sun and lack of relatives made it far more appealing to Maia than her childhood home.

"Maia, darling!"

Petite, vivacious Julia Foy must have seen Maia from the house, for she appeared through the open french windows and ran heavily but still gracefully down the verandah and across the rolling green lawn to embrace Maia with enthusiasm.

"Julia!" Maia cried, trying to be gentle in her return hug. "Should you really be running right now?"

Julia rolled her blue eyes and rested a hand on her rounded stomach. "Oh, you're worse than Daniel. You'd think Queen Victoria was still on the throne, the way he fusses at me to rest and put my feet up. I'm fine, I promise. I feel stronger than I ever have in my life! Impatient for August, though. I want to meet this little one."

Julia linked her arm through Maia's and they walked to the house at a more sedate pace, Maia shortening her stride to match her friend's smaller steps. Julia was full of questions about life in London, Ellie's wedding dress and the dresses of the wedding party, why Maia wasn't a bridesmaid, the guest list for the wedding, and why Maia didn't have a beau of her own after eight months in the city.

"I didn't move in with Aunt Amelia to meet men," Maia said to this last in exasperation.

Julia glanced sideways at her. "It doesn't seem like you, I agree, but as you never gave a proper reason for why you were going, what is one to think?"

Guilt twisted Maia's stomach. People who were not able to work magic had to be kept in ignorance of its existence, by law. She hated keeping her new life a secret from her friend, but she had no choice.

It must have been worse for Julia's husband Dan. A weather magician, he could not tell his wife anything about his work or that part of his life. If their child proved to have magical abilities, that too would have to be covered up or disguised for Julia.

Maia didn't think she could bear keeping something that important from a spouse—but Dan never seemed too bothered by it, nor did Aunt Amelia or any of Maia's new magician friends see anything odd or uncomfortable about it.

People were funny.

"It's hard to give a clear reason," she said now, picking her way carefully through her words. "I suppose, really, it came down to wanting a chance to be myself, away from my family. To learn what I am capable of."

"France wasn't enough for you?"

Maia's memory called up an image of Julia in the distinctive blue-and-white VAD uniform, face streaked with mud and blood, all traces of vivacity buried under calm efficiency as she assisted Dr. Smythe in amputating a soldier's mangled leg.

As soon as the war ended, Julia married that soldier, Sergeant Daniel Foy.

"The war showed me what I could do in a crisis. I needed to learn who and what I could be during peacetime."

"And have you figured it out?"

Maia thought of her lessons with her aunt, how she was learning to harness and use her magical ability, the wonders that were starting to unfold before her.

"I think I'm starting to," she said.

Julia squeezed her arm in silent understanding.

***

Maia was reluctant to leave the relative serenity of Little Oaks for the formal family dinner at Stanbury that evening. At least Julia and Dan, as close friends of both the bride and groom, were coming as well. Maia did not have to endure her family alone.

Due to Dan's false leg and Julia's condition, walking to Stanbury was out of the question. The Foys had a Crossley tourer, one of the latest models, mostly to satisfy Julia's craze for automobiles. Maia did not know much about autos, nor did she care, but she made appreciative noises as Julia described the inner workings and outer trappings of the Crossley with as much enthusiasm as though it were her own child.

Julia was an excellent driver, if fast, and the three arrived safe, sound, and windblown on Stanbury's doorstep right on time.

"Oh," said Ellie by way of greeting as they entered the front hall, where a crowd of mostly young people milled. "Maia. What an ... interesting frock."

For once, the sneer did not get under Maia's skin. One of her new London friends was a journeyman magician with an impeccable eye for fashion. Helen had helped Maia to pick her wardrobe for this trip, and Maia's faith in her judgement was firm.

She doubted that Ellie actually disliked the frock, or even felt particularly jealous. Ellie's own dress was the latest style from London, gorgeously bedizened and styled. Spiteful comments to put Maia in her place were nothing more than a habit with Ellie.

"Hello, Electra," Julia said, loudly and pointedly.

Ellie jumped and belatedly remembered her manners. "Oh—hello Julia, hello Dan. Freddie—"

She dug an elbow in her fiancé's side. The Honorable Frederick Winters dragged himself away from a conversation with one of the Rawlings cousins, and turned to greet the newcomers.

"Hullo Foy, dashed good of you to come. Julia, lookin' positively radiant, if I may be allowed to say it. Maia, glad you could tear yourself away from dear old London for this. I say, that is a smart thingummy you've got on. My sister will want to know where you got it—ho, Jen! Come see Maia's frock!"

Ellie's face pinched into a sour expression. Jennifer Moreau *nee* Winters, married to a Frenchman and living in Paris, was the most stylish woman at the dinner. If she approved Maia's dress, Ellie could hardly maintain the illusion it was frumpy.

Maia reflected once again that the Whitney family was by far getting the best of this marriage. Freddie's family was profligate and poor, and Freddie himself not the brightest, but he was a dear, kind soul. Ellie ... was not.

Jen walked over in a rustle of silk. "Hullo, everyone," she said, smiling coolly and impartially over the entire group.

More guests had arrived by now, so by unspoken consent their group moved away from the entryway, leaving Ellie and

Freddie to continue their greeting duties.

"Freddie is right, that is a charming frock, Maia," Jen said, studying it carefully. "Is it French?"

"English," Maia said with no little pride.

Her friend Helen had started with a simple sage green silk slip right from the shop, and then had covered it with her own embellishments, using just a touch of magic to enhance the end result. The silver embroidery was hardly noticeable until the light reflected off it, and then it shimmered like water under the moon.

Maia's magical aura, visible only when she worked magic and then only to herself, was silver, so she found the dress particularly appropriate as well as stunning.

"Well, you must introduce me to your dressmaker," Jen said.

"Speaking of stunning, your bracelet is remarkable," Julia said. Dan's eyes glazed over and he limped away from this feminine conversation. "Is it a family heirloom?"

The ruby-and-gold construction around Jen's wrist did draw the eye. Maia was surprised Ellie had bothered to notice her dress when there was a piece of jewelry of this sort to be envied. It matched the deep crimson of Jen's dress and set off her dark hair and eyes, making her the center of attention in any room she entered.

"Isn't it gorgeous? Jacques bought it for me. It's not an heirloom yet, but we hope it will be eventually."

Before the war, speaking openly about starting a family heirloom collection might have been considered déclassé—if one's family wasn't ancient and established enough to already have pieces a hundred years in the safe, one had no business acquiring such now.

But times were changing. Daniel Foy bought Little Oaks to be his family estate with only a few local murmurings about social climbers and interlopers. Jen and Jacques could consider starting family traditions for their children and grandchildren in the same way they were setting about rebuilding France.

Maia wasn't sure she was quite ready for the brave new world her sister Merry's Socialism strove for, but neither did she have any desire to return to the life of the past—one full of empty rituals and devoid of purpose.

In her case, devoid of magic as well.

Loren, the butler hired for the occasion, stepped into the hallway.

"Your pardon, miss," he said to Maia. "Your mother wishes me to inform you that dinner is served."

Maia offered him a cool smile. "Thank you, Mr. Loren, but I believe my mother forgot I am not responsible for the evening's activities. It's my sister Ellie—Miss Electra—you should be telling."

His bland face moved not a muscle. "Indeed."

As he moved toward Ellie and Freddie, Julia laughed. "Your mother is determined to put you in charge of this weekend, isn't she?"

"Not half so determined as I to avoid that fate," Maia said, with her smile still in place.

Ellie's voice rose shrilly above the cultured babble of the crowd, fussing at Loren that they were supposed to have cocktails before dinner. Maia had to prick her ears to hear his wooden response that Mrs. Whitney had said nothing about any of that to him, miss.

"Oh, all right," Ellie finally said in a huff, while Freddie grimaced apologetically at Loren. "Everyone, it's time to eat."

Maia knew there had been a fierce debate between Mrs. Whitney and Ellie over whether they would have a wedding breakfast or a light tea after the ceremony, with Ellie wishing to prove to the groom's titled family that she could be just as fashionable as they, and Mrs. Whitney insisting that people expected a proper sit-down breakfast after a wedding and that was what they would get.

Mrs. Whitney had won that argument by virtue of Ellie being incapable of keeping her temper and sticking to the point in a verbal spat.

It seemed their mother had claimed this victory as well, through Ellie's refusal to deal directly with the staff herself.

Maia was thankful to be outside it all.

Ellie did not share her feelings.

As the bride and groom proceeded into the dining room, Ellie shot her sister a poisonous glare and hissed, "This is all your fault! If you cared an ounce for me, you'd have helped me get my own way instead of leaving me to deal with Mama on my own!"

Maia was too well-bred to roll her eyes, but it was a near thing.

***

They survived the meal and had gathered in the drawing room after, some people talking about leaving or heading upstairs to their rooms so they could be sure of getting enough sleep before the big day tomorrow, when Jen put her hand to her wrist and said—

"Oh! I've lost my bracelet."

There was a flurry of movement as everyone instinctively

looked down, around, and in some cases, up. No one spotted the sparkling scarlet and gold circle.

"Perhaps it slipped its catch and fell off in the dining room," Jacques suggested.

Jen, looking washed-out and unhappy, agreed that must have been what happened, and returned to the dining room to check.

Jacques tried to cover the mildly uneasy air that had fallen over the company by saying he knew he shouldn't have trusted that jeweler to tighten the clasp properly—the man had red hair, and everyone knew red-headed people were shifty.

Since red hair in all its various shades ran in the Whitney family, this joke fell flat among that half of the party. Maia's own hair was more brown than red, but even she felt a touch of annoyance on behalf of her few auburn strands.

Jen returned with a crease in her forehead and worry in her eyes. "It wasn't there," she said.

The unease grew worse as everyone scattered to hunt for it in earnest, Jen apologizing to all and sundry for being such a nuisance, Mrs. Whitney ordering the staff to search in every corner and leave no stone unturned, Ellie's face growing more and more petulant as less and less attention was given to the bride and diverted instead to the groom's sister.

She came around the side of the sofa where Maia was checking under the cushions, grabbed Maia's arm, and dragged her out of the drawing room and into Mr. Whitney's study.

Maia rubbed where Ellie's rounded nails had dug in. "Ow."

Ellie ignored her. "Fix this!"

"Oh, for heaven's sake."

Ellie ignored this as well. "If that bracelet isn't found at once, my wedding will always be remembered as the occasion where Jen lost her bracelet, not anything to do with me at all! It will be a blot on my entire married life with Freddie! I'll be a social pariah! No one will ever want to come to my dinner parties: 'Oh, well, I'm sure it wasn't her fault, but you know, my dear, one doesn't quite like to take the chance ...' I'll be ruined! I know you don't care about me at all now you're an elegant Londoner, but surely you still have some sisterly feeling in what's left of your heart." Ellie sniffed and put a tiny handkerchief to her kohl-lined eyes.

Maia winced. "Must you be so dramatic? You'll end up just like Mama if you aren't careful."

Ellie's green eyes flashed at that accusation, but there was little she could say in response without proving it true.

"What is it you want me to do, anyway?" Maia continued.

Ellie stamped her foot in its ridiculous high-heeled silver shoe. "Clearly, one of the servants must have seen the thing and pocketed it after it fell off Jen's wrist at dinner. It's ostentatious enough, the gaudy thing. Find out which one took it, fire him or her, and get the wretched bauble back to Jen without any more fuss!"

Merry slipped into the study in time to hear that. "How dare you accuse the servants like that, just because they're a lower class? That is so typical of people like you. It's much more likely one of your friends took it as a dare, or someone in Freddie's family needed to pay off gambling debts."

Ellie rounded on her. "None of my so-called posh friends are here tonight, it's only family and old friends, and *nobody* in Freddie's family gambles anymore since what happened to his father and older brother! Are you going to tell me Uncle

William took it, or old Mrs. Croft?"

"I wouldn't put it past Cousin Arabella," Merry said cynically.

That stopped Ellie in her tracks. "Frankly, neither would I," she admitted, an errant dimple showing briefly in her cheek before she remembered to bring her scowl back.

"All right," Maia said quietly.

Both sisters stopped and looked at her.

"What?" Ellie said.

"I'll look into it." Maia bit back a sigh.

For all her insistence she wouldn't get involved in her family's drama, here she was. She didn't see how she could refuse this time, though. It wasn't just Ellie, it was for Jen's sake as well.

Besides, as over-dramatic as Ellie was, she had a point. Society could be cruel and gossip spread like wildfire. People would be quick to use this incident, harmless or not, against Ellie and Freddie. Despite what Ellie thought, Maia did care for her sister. She didn't want to see her hurt over something that wasn't her fault.

Suffering she brought on herself, that was her own burden to carry.

"You'll make whichever servant stole it give it back?" Ellie asked.

Merry folded her arms across her front. "I insist you question the guests as well if you question the servants. I will not stand for class injustice in my own home!"

Maia held out her hands. "If you want me to take care of this, you'll have to let me do it my way. Don't worry, I haven't been living with Aunt Amelia long enough to have picked up her tactlessness."

That got a faint smile from both sisters, as she'd hoped.

"I'll do it as smoothly and fairly as possible. Merry, I will question the servers first, not because I think they're more likely to have taken the bracelet but rather that they are more likely to have seen what happened to it. Ellie, if you could ask Dan and Uncle William to come see me, as they were on either side of Jen, I will ask them what they observed, as well. Hopefully that will get us to the bottom of this without stepping on any toes."

Or without having to search all the guests and staff and make outright accusations.

This time Maia did sigh. "And somebody had better discreetly check Cousin Arabella's handbag, just in case."

Even now, she was more than half convinced they were making a mountain out of a molehill. Cousin Arabella's fondness for bright trinkets notwithstanding, Maia couldn't believe they were entertaining a thief in their midst, be it staff or guest.

It simply wasn't done, stealing during a wedding celebration. No, it had to be a mistake.

Maia stayed in the study, as it was a convenient place to question people and she didn't think her father would have a chance to sneak off to hide in it tonight. Her sisters left, Ellie to find the guests Maia had requested, Merry to bring in (and probably warn) the hired staff who had been serving at the table.

First in was Loren, holding himself as stiffly as ever.

"Ah, Mr. Loren, just the person to help me," Maia said, smiling at him.

His face didn't move, his eyes trained somewhere above her head.

Likely he despised them for having a hire a temporary butler for this affair rather than keeping one on permanently. Maia thought it a ridiculous affectation herself, but her mother and Ellie wanted to present the best possible picture of their family to all their guests and, more importantly, Freddie's family.

She persevered. "As you know, Madame Moreau has lost her bracelet and we can't find it anywhere. I am hoping to draw a better picture of where and how it might have got lost by talking to everyone who saw it during the meal."

"Are you accusing one of my staff of taking it, Miss Whitney?"

Maia narrowed her eyes and lifted her chin at him. "That's quite the conclusion to which to jump, Mr. Loren. Why would you think so, when my words so clearly indicate otherwise?"

For the first time, he looked at her face. "From what Miss Merope let drop ..."

This time, Maia did roll her eyes. "My sister Merry shares the family tendency to exaggerate," she said. "I assure you, I do not. All I want to know is when was the last time you noticed the bracelet on Madame Moreau's wrist, and if you saw anything unusual in the dining room at any point."

There was a brief pause. Then—

"I cannot remember anything, miss."

If his quick leap to the defensive hadn't already made her suspicious, this would have. Still, unless she wanted to outright accuse him of lying, she had to let him go and wait for the next person.

The first waiter said he'd noticed Madame Moreau's bracelet when she picked up her spoon for the soup course, but couldn't say for certain if she'd had it on after that or not, he hadn't been paying close attention, sorry, miss.

The next hadn't noticed the bracelet at all, miss, but he could tell her that Madame Moreau's wrist was empty as she lifted her glass to finish the last of her wine right before they all rose from the table, because he remembered thinking how odd it was that a stylish lady like that wouldn't be wearing any jewelry.

"So the bracelet disappeared sometime in between the soup course and the end of the meal," Maia said, making a note. "Thank you, that is an enormous help."

The rest of the wait staff corroborated this in various ways, but nobody could narrow it down any further. Maia sent Merry to ask Mrs. Tate if they'd found the bracelet in any of the dishes returned to the kitchen, in the unlikely case it had fallen into Jen's soup bowl or some other far-fetched notion.

Merry returned with a decided negative, and Maia reluctantly began her task of questioning the guests.

First in was her mother's brother, Uncle William Rawlings, who had been seated on Jen's left side. He was considerably younger than both Mrs. Whitney and Aunt Amelia, and considered himself a dashing buck.

All three Whitney sisters dreaded his visits as he insisted on teasing them about beaux and flirtations and treating them as though they lived in a Victorian novel.

"I say, bad show this, what?" he blustered, dropping into the chair set before Mr. Whitney's desk. "I say, Maia, this is no work for you. Your father ought to be organizing these questions while you are out dancing with the fellows and maybe planning your wedding next, eh? Can't let both your younger sisters beat you, after all. You don't want to end up an old maid like Amelia, do you?"

Maia gritted her teeth and smiled. "Now, now, Uncle William, you know I'm living with Aunt Amelia now, so you mustn't say naughty things about her. What I really want to know," hurrying before he could insert another comment, "is did you notice Madame Moreau's bracelet at all during the meal? We think it must have come off then, so we're trying to pin down exactly when it fell off and where it ended up."

"'Course I saw the da—er, the dratted thing! Flashed in my eyes every time she lifted her fork or took a drink. The thing was half mesmerizing, I couldn't seem to take my eyes off it, not until I turned away to chat with my neighbor on the other side. By the time I turned back, it didn't bother me so much."

He stopped and rubbed his chin. For all their quirks, no one could accuse any of the Rawlings of stupidity. "No. Dash it, it was gone! I was so relieved not to have it filling my gaze I didn't take note. Now, ain't that a peculiar thing?"

Relief surged in Maia's breast. She was getting somewhere at last!

"Very strange. Do you remember when it was you turned to talk to your other neighbor, and when you turned back?"

It turned out Uncle William had started chatting with his left-hand neighbor somewhere around the meat course and turned back to do his duty by Jen for the dessert.

"And you didn't notice anything unusual during any of it?"

He stroked his chin again. "I will say that Madame Moreau seemed more tired during the pudding. Not that she looked poorly, mind you—wouldn't do to say that about a lady." He winked roguishly. "But—the only way I can put it is that she seemed larger-than-life at the start of the meal, and more like an ordinary lady by the end."

He huffed a faint laugh. "Seems like nonsense, but there you have it. Now, you finish up this task and get back to doing what pretty girls ought to do—flirting and getting your beauty sleep for tomorrow!"

For once, Maia didn't mind his abysmal raillery. He had given her a tremendous clue.

"Thank you, Uncle William," she said mechanically.

He winked again and left.

What if *Jen* stole her own bracelet? What if it was insured, and she needed the money for something? Merry's nasty crack about the Winters' gambling habits returned to mind.

Freddie's father and eldest brother had all but ruined the family with their gambling debts. The shame of their reputation had seemed to give the rest of the siblings an abhorrence of debt, but what if Jen was more like them than anyone realized?

Was that why she looked so unhappy after it went missing, because she felt guilty?

It didn't make sense that she would choose her brother's wedding party to perform the theft. It wasn't like her to be so callous—

Ah. Maia had it. If it happened anywhere else, Jacques might be suspicious, or an innocent person might be blamed. Here, it could remain an unsolved mystery.

"One of the hired staff must have taken it," they could say, but since nothing could be proven and the staff would soon be moving on to new work, no one would live with an unjust accusation. Or if worse came to worst, they could always shrug and murmur something about poor old Cousin Arabella, and that would be the end of it.

As much as Maia liked Jen, she would not let her use Ellie's wedding like that. Ellie was her sister, and that was the end of it. Apparently blood really was thicker than water.

Maia carried on her questioning with renewed vigor, hoping to find proof she could use to confront Jen, rather than a tenuous theory.

To her joy, Dan was the next person in.

"You were seated on the other side of Jen?" she asked.

Due to the Whitney tendency toward producing girls rather than boys, the numbers had been uneven at dinner, and so Maia had been placed between Freddie's Aunt Myrtle and her second cousin Cecily Whitney down toward the foot of the table. Between complaints from Aunt Myrtle about her lumbago and ungrateful relatives (Maia was not always sure which was which) and whining from Cousin Cecily about the lack of young men since the war, Maia had had little opportunity to see anything around her.

"I was," he agreed, leaning back in the chair and massaging his leg stump. "And yes, I noticed the bracelet at the beginning of the meal. All I could think of when I looked at it was how much I'd love to get something like that for Julia. But I promise, I didn't steal it for her."

He grinned wryly.

Maia smiled back. "You are the last person I'd suspect of something like that, Dan. I am glad to have you here nonetheless. Tell me, are there any spells we could use to locate the wretched thing?"

He shrugged. "Absolutely, if you are willing to either clear out the entire household or reveal the existence of magic to everyone here."

Her shoulders slumped. "I was afraid of that. It would

have made things too easy."

"Sorry," he said.

Maia straightened back up. "We'll have to continue with old-fashioned detective work. I don't suppose you saw anything of value?"

"Sorry," he said again. "The bracelet made me think of Julia, and then about the—the baby, and whether it would be a boy or a girl, and ..." His expression shifted into distant warmth.

"I understand," Maia said, spreading her hands wide on the desk top. "Only another couple of months now."

He shifted his weight in the chair. "Julia wants a boy, to carry on the family name, but I'm hoping for a girl, one just like her mother. Little Oaks is mine to do as I please with, I can settle it on my firstborn even if it isn't a boy."

He stopped and shook his head. "None of which is relevant to your problem. Have you talked to the maid?"

Maia frowned. "What maid? Mother only wanted male staff to serve. She said a maid waiting tables was improper."

Dan lifted his eyebrows. "All I know is, I dropped my napkin at one point and a maid scurried past and scooped it up, then brought me a fresh one."

"Hm," said Maia. "Nobody mentioned a maid. I'll have to see what I can find. Thank you, Dan."

After Loren had returned and insisted no maids were at work in the dining room, by Mrs. Whitney's express order, an exasperated Maia had no choice but to call the female hired staff in one by one and interview them each separately.

At this rate, she wouldn't finish the task until the wedding was long over.

She sent a note to Ellie saying she was getting through as

quickly as possible, but they might want to start a game or something to distract the guests from the fact that no one could leave yet.

The first three maids gave no new information, but the fourth trembled and burst into tears when Maia asked if she'd been in the dining room at all during the meal.

"Oh miss—I mean, no miss, not at all," she said unconvincingly, twisting a handkerchief between shaking fingers.

Maia held onto the last shreds of her patience.

"I'm not cross, Daisy," she said. "I simply need to know what happened."

Daisy leaned forward and buried her face in her hands, sobbing incoherently. Maia passed her a clean handkerchief to replace the sodden one she held and waited for the storm to pass.

Eventually it all came out.

Mr. Loren had carried out the wrong bottle of wine to go with the pudding, so Daisy had scurried after him with the correct one to make the change before he poured. On her way back to the kitchen, she had noticed a napkin on the floor. When she picked it up, she saw Madame Moreau's bracelet beneath it.

"I promise, miss, I picked it up to return to her, I really did! But once I held it in my hand, I—I—I've never held anything so lovely in my life, miss. I couldn't give it up."

Maia didn't know whether to be relieved or disappointed. Her brilliant theory was wrong, but Jen's character remained unstained.

Merry would be furious that it was a servant after all.

"It was wrong of you, Daisy, but as I can see you are sorry,

27

give it back to me and I'll return it to Madame Moreau with nothing more said about it."

The maid's eyes widened. "But—I thought you understood, miss. I don't have it anymore."

"What?"

It turned out that Daisy's conscience had gotten the best of her. After the pudding course, as the guests were leaving the table, she dropped it in the entryway between the dining room and front hall so that someone would notice it to return to Madame Moreau, and nobody would ever have to know she took it.

"Only nobody did, and it's still missing," Maia groaned.

She extracted a list of the guests milling around that entryway when Daisy dropped the bracelet and sent the girl on her way with a stern warning to never give in to temptation again, lest she find herself in a worse position than this.

Now for more guests.

Maia's hair was carefully coiffed and pinned for the evening, so she resisted the urge to clutch at it. The temptation was strong, though.

Why had she agreed to do this? As embarrassing as it would have been for her parents and Ellie, she ought to have insisted they call in Ray Andrews—Detective Sergeant Andrews, to give him his proper title—and have him handle the matter instead. This sort of thing was Ray's job, not hers.

Alas, she had let family feeling overcome her common sense, and now she was stuck with it. Sighing, she checked the list of names Daisy had given her and went to the door to ask Freddie's cousin Bertie for a word.

Like Daisy before him, Bertie shuffled his feet, twisted his hands, and craned his neck to look up at the ceiling in a blatant attempt to avoid Maia's eyes. As her handkerchief was still wet from Daisy's tears, Maia was only thankful he didn't start sobbing as well.

"All right, Bertie, out with it," she said, adopting the no-nonsense tone of command she had used on recalcitrant soldiers in the ward during the war. "You either saw or did something, so tell me now and let's get this matter settled so everyone can go to bed."

"It's not my fault," he said automatically, moistening his lips.

Which meant, of course, that it absolutely was.

"I won't know whether it's your fault or not until you tell me what 'it' is," Maia pointed out.

"It's this girl, see," he said.

Of course it was.

"Girls aren't like they used to be, they require a fellow prove he loves them with gifts, dinners, fancy parties, that sort of thing. I know gambling is wrong, goodness knows we've all had it dinned in our ears since we were shavers to not end up like Freddie's pater, but I thought, well, horses aren't like real gambling. So I put some down on a sure thing, only it wasn't. Then I thought I could make it up with the next race, only that one lost too, and well, you know how it is."

"I don't," Maia said. She was in no mood to pretend sympathy for irresponsible and foolhardy behavior.

"Oh. Well, there you are. The girl left me for some richer chap, and I was left with this pile of debts. My father wouldn't cover me, since gambling is the cardinal sin in this family, y'know, so I was in a hole. And there you are."

"So when you saw Jen's bracelet on the floor on your way out of the dining room you decided to steal it and sell it to pay off your debts?" Maia couldn't quite keep the scorn from her voice.

"It wasn't like that! I was going to return it to her, honest. Only I got thinking about all those debts, and how Jacques ain't exactly poor and it was probably insured and it wasn't like it was a family heirloom anyway, and then I thought if I pawned it, I could redeem it and return it to her once my luck turned."

Maia held out her hand. "I'm sure you see I cannot let you do that, but if you give it back to me now I think we can let the matter drop."

He stared. "I can't do that."

"Whyever not?"

"Because I don't have it anymore. Someone lifted it right out of my pocket without me noticing."

Maia's heart sank. "You don't know who?"

"Haven't the foggiest. Didn't even know it was gone until you asked me to come in and I patted my pocket to check on it. Sorry."

Maia groaned aloud and laid her head down on the desk.

***

Maia called in Ellie, Freddie, Mrs. Whitney, Jen, and Jacques, and explained the situation to them.

"So you see," she ended, "the only thing we can do now is turn the matter over to the police. I'm at the end of my resources."

"No!" cried Ellie. "May, I thought you understood how important this was to me. I thought you *cared*!"

Mrs. Whitney rested the back of her hand on her forehead. "Alas, that it should come to this. Police in my house! The shame to our family honor ... this is a stain time will ne'er erase."

Everyone ignored her.

"Ellie, I said I'd try. I've done my best, but this is beyond me."

Ellie pouted and glared. Freddie patted her hand.

"Can't be helped, I suppose," he said. "Dashed sorry about this, Jen."

Jen shook her head. "No, I'm sorry. I'm beginning to think that dratted bracelet is under a curse. Jacques, you remember the trouble we got into with it in Cannes? And that would-be thief on the train? I suppose we must find the thief, but I almost feel that it's more trouble than it's worth."

"It is we who must apologize to you, Mme Whitney, for bringing such trouble to your door," Jacques said in his heavy accent, bowing slightly in Mrs. Whitney's direction.

Maia barely registered this. Her mind worked furiously. Could it be ...?

She stood up.

"Excuse me a moment," she said. "I must speak to someone. I'll be right back."

In the drawing room, where the guests listlessly played bridge or carried on desultory conversations with each other while Mr. Whitney snoozed openly in his overstuffed chair, Maia grabbed Dan and dragged him into the hallway.

"Daniel! Is it possible that bracelet has ..." she lowered her voice, even though no one could overhear them in this spot, "a spell on it? Some sort of attraction spell, to draw everyone's attention and make people desire it for themselves?"

Everything would make sense then. Why Jen looked so pale and peaked after she lost the bracelet—she was no longer basking in its enchanted glow. Why it was all anyone could see or think about when they saw it on her wrist, and why so many people were tempted to steal it.

Surely no other explanation would suffice for three thieves—at least!—in one evening, not to mention all the other incidents Jen had mentioned.

Dan raised his eyebrows. "That's outside my realm of expertise, but it's certainly possible. But how does that help you find it?"

"Oh." Maia deflated. "I hadn't thought of that."

She had been so certain this had solved her problem.

"In fact," Dan said. "If it is enchanted, that might make things more difficult. Who knows if the police themselves would be able to resist its lure?"

"So I daren't call them in after all. Ellie will be pleased."

"Not necessarily. There's an entire division of Deep dedicated to recovering enchanted objects and removing said enchantment. They'll have to send someone out at once."

"Domestic Protection! Dan, I can't!"

She hadn't been a magician's apprentice for a full year, but already she knew that Domestic Protection—the agency that took care of minor magical infractions in Great Britain—was not someone you wanted visiting your home. To have a matter not serious enough for Magical Intelligence but beyond one's ability to handle oneself was a mark of disfavor within the magical community.

The Deep agents themselves, aware of their unpopularity, tended to be surly and even downright rude. They would not spare the feelings of anyone involved, no matter how innocent.

"It isn't terribly likely," Dan tried to reassure her. "Deep has records of most enchanted objects, and usually keeps track of them all. If Jen's bracelet really was bespelled, they ought to have known about it from the moment it entered the country, and sent someone to keep a discreet eye on it."

"But how—"

Oh. *Oh*. Now *that* made sense.

Dan's eyes twinkled. "I take it you've solved the crime?"

The weight of exhaustion lifted from Maia's shoulders, and she smiled brilliantly back at him. "Do you know, I believe I have."

Unlike her theory of Jen's guilt, this fit all the pieces together and left nothing unexplained. Maia had never admired Mr. Sherlock Holmes, but now she understood the sense of satisfaction he felt at an elegant solution which only he could have concocted and which was undoubtedly correct.

"Mr. Loren!" she called, seeing the hired butler cross the drawing room. "Can I have a word?"

Not betraying discomposure by so much as a twist of an eyebrow or purse of the mouth, he sailed to join them.

"Shall I leave?" Dan asked.

"Not at all," Maia said.

She suspected she might need a witness for this.

"Mr. Loren, if you have quite finished cleaning up the bracelet, I would like to return it to Madame Moreau," she said.

Dan's jaw dropped.

Loren, finally, showed some expression. He raised his eyebrows.

"I beg your pardon, miss?"

"Oh come, it's obvious. You are a terrible butler, even for one hired for the occasion. The wrong wine for the pudding?

Telling me that dinner was served rather than my sister? Even if my mother had instructed you to do so, any butler worth his salt would have 'misheard' her direction and told the proper person instead. Your inability to remember anything from the meal?

"Not only that, you lied to me when you said no maid had been in the dining room. Daisy entered to save you from pouring the wrong wine during the pudding course."

"Perhaps I only wanted to save her from accusations such as the one you are making to me," he said.

Maia shook her head. "Oh no. You caused the clasp to loosen on the bracelet and covered it with Dan's napkin so no one else would see it until you had a chance to pocket it. That's what distracted you enough to choose the incorrect wine."

It was simple enough magic to slide open a gold jewelry clasp and cause a linen napkin to succumb to gravity.

"Unfortunately for you, Daisy picked up the napkin and saw the bracelet, then had an attack of conscience and dropped it again before you could take it from her. You saw Bertie Winters pocket it and took it from him at your first opportunity. You've had plenty of time to do what needed to be done with it, so I would like it back."

"How do you know I do not want to keep it for myself?"

Maia smiled her most patient smile at him. "Mr. Loren, I am quite certain that a proper thief would never have made the mistakes you did. Only the rankest amateur would slip up so much."

He heaved a sigh, and suddenly his face relaxed into the semblance of a human being.

"Cor, and ain't I glad to be done with this job."

He delved into his pocket and passed the bracelet to Maia, who was happy to note no sense of desire or covetousness as it came into her possession.

"It's been a right slip-up from the start. Deep was supposed to clear up the problems with this little piece on the train, but the fool of a fellow they sent muffed it. I got stuck with this job and let me tell you, it ain't been all beer and skittles! Though I must say, no one else noticed my mistakes 'cept you, miss. You ain't looking for a job, are you?"

Maia laughed. "Thank you, no."

"So it was enchanted?" Dan demanded. The mention of Deep meant they no longer had to use oblique references to magic; they were one and all part of the magical community.

"Remnants of an old charm," this new Loren said, wiping sweat off his brow with a plain, cheap handkerchief. If Maia had seen *that* earlier she would have tumbled to his identity even sooner. "In its heyday, people would've killed for that trinket. Now it just exerts a strong draw on the weak-minded or those who might already want such a thing."

"Thank goodness Cousin Arabella was seated at the other end of the table, then," Maia said, mostly to herself.

"I'd say human greed was more to blame for tonight's events than a spell, but I removed what was left. It's safe enough to return to the French lady."

"And what shall I tell her?" Maia demanded.

Loren shrugged. "Not my problem, miss."

Dan surprised them both by bursting into laughter.

"Sorry," he said, covering his mouth. "It's just—Maia, you can tell them the butler did it!"

Many Magical

Returns

Susanna glared at the blood-spotted handkerchief in her lap as she pulled the sharp needle out of her thumb yet again. Would Mother notice if she used magic to clean the blood and finish the hemstitching? A glance across the stuffy parlor with its dreary brown-and-buff wallpaper at her mother's pinched lips and narrowed eyes assured the girl that she would.

Lowering her eyes in a semblance of meekness, Susanna pressed her thumb into the palm of her other hand until the bleeding stopped, and attempted another stitch.

At least no blood had dropped onto her dress. They had lost another maid this week. Susanna did not fancy trying to get blood out of her pale grey poplin without the use of even a simple stain-removal spell, the kind any laundress worth her salt could use in her sleep.

The injustice of Mother's refusal to allow her to practice magic rankled more than ever today. Today, Susanna Westwood turned seventeen years old, a proper young lady at last.

Father would have made a fuss; he'd always loved celebrations. Not Mother. She hadn't even bothered to wish Susanna many happy returns of the day.

Uncle Ernie had mentioned the day over breakfast, but only to joke that soon Susanna would be marrying and leaving them.

As if she wanted a husband! All Susanna wanted—all she'd ever wanted, her entire life, was to be a magician. Oh, a family might be nice someday, but not for years yet.

After Father's death, though, Mother refused to let Susanna use her magic. She'd even gone so far as to tell Uncle

Ernie that Susanna and Ned had both lost their abilities through grief over their father's unexpected demise.

Susanna was thankful for her brother, who did not forget about her even after he escaped to Harrow, and then Cambridge. It was Ned who passed along spells and cantrips, along with his tutors' instructions in the proper use of magic. Thanks to his letters, written in the sibings' private code to avoid prying eyes, Susanna had been able to practice her magic at night in the privacy of her bedroom, with the curtains drawn and a towel stuffed under the door to keep anyone from seeing the golden-green light of her magic.

Magic could not be taught openly at public schools, of course, not if the magicians of the world wished to keep themselves in safe seclusion, but there were always a few tutors posted at universities to keep an eye out for magically-inclined students and give them private tutorials.

Susanna, trapped at home with her mother and uncle, had no such luck.

"Susanna!" Mother snapped. "Pay attention!"

Susanna blinked and looked down. While letting her thoughts wander, she had inadvertently stitched the handkerchief to the skirt of her dress.

Mother continued chiding. "Honestly, after all I have taught you, all the money we have spent on governesses, and you are still a flighty, irresponsible child. Seventeen years of age and no more sense than an infant. Any twelve-year-old girl could make a better job of that handkerchief! At your age you should be far beyond such simple projects, but no, your head is too full of fancies and nonsense. Furthermore—"

She got no further. Susanna lunged to her feet, the attached handkerchief dangling awkwardly from the front of her skirt. "Of course I can't take things seriously when you refuse to allow me to do anything real! If you would only allow me to practice my magic—"

"Hush!" Mother said, her glare freezing Susanna to her very bones.

Uncle Ernie bustled in from the library, newspaper in hand. "Here now, what's all the fuss?" he said with a scowl. "Can't a man read his paper in peace without being interrupted by feminine quarrels?"

"It's nothing, Ernie," Mother said hastily. "Susanna, go to your room."

Susanna seethed. She was fed up with being dismissed and treated as a child, never given a chance.

"It is not nothing!" she cried. "I am seventeen years old and a magician, Mother, or I could be if you would trust me. If you won't let me practice my magic, I'll find someone who will!"

"Hold your tongue, you disgraceful girl!" Mother began, face white above the drab brown of her high-collared frock.

This time it was Uncle Ernie who interrupted.

"A magician, hey?" he said, looking Susanna up and down as though seeing her for the first time. "Helen, you told me her magic had vanished the day her father died."

"It did—she has delusions of grandeur, that's all," Mother said, hands pressed together in front on her. For the first time that Susanna could remember, her unemotional voice shook.

Susanna threw her head back. "It did not," she said through clenched teeth. "Look!"

She banished all thought of her mother from her mind so she could concentrate, focusing on the stitches holding the handkerchief to her dress. She whispered the Latin incantation for release, and the thread curled back onto itself, freeing the handkerchief to fall to the floor.

"Susanna!" Mother said, and Susanna had never heard her voice so shrill. "Stop this at once!"

"No, no," Uncle Ernie said, smooth as silk. "Pray continue, girl."

Susanna had no intention of stopping now. She was too intoxicated with the glorious joy of using her magic freely for the first time in twelve years to quit.

She called the handkerchief to her hand and spoke the words to free it of bloodstains. Next she set the needle and thread in place and enchanted them to finish the stitching without aid from her. Her final act was to summon up a glamour, making her dull, old-maidish frock appear the clinging, frothy, golden-yellow dress of her dreams. She couldn't change it in reality, but she was very good at making things seem other than they were.

Uncle Ernie watched the process with narrowed eyes. Mother, hovering in the background with one hand supporting her on the back of the settee, bit her lip but said nothing more.

As the glamour settled into place, Susanna snipped the thread and handed the handkerchief to her uncle. "There!"

"Impressive," he said, inspecting it. "Can you do anything besides small magic?"

"Yes," she said recklessly. "And if I received proper training, I could do more yet."

The words "proper training" recalled the first lesson of magic. She hastily added, "*Finiatur.*" A magician never left a spell hanging.

The spells ended but the glamour stayed in place. Once

set, it was self-sustaining for several hours.

Mother moaned and buried her face in her hands.

Uncle Ernie raised his eyebrows. "Helen," turning to Mother with a swift frown. "I believe you've been deceiving me all these years."

Mother raised her head. Her cheeks were white, but there was a fire in her eyes Susanna hadn't seen before. For the first time, Susanna felt a trickle of unease.

There was something going on here beyond her understanding. What had she unleashed?

"I won't let you take her," Mother said to Uncle Ernie. "I won't let you use her as you used me."

Use Susanna? Used Mother? Susanna didn't understand this at all.

Uncle Ernie smiled. A shiver ran down Susanna's spine. She had never seen her dandyish uncle look so menacing.

"Do you know, Helen, I really don't think you can stop me." He rubbed his hands together. "The timing is perfect. I've been contacted by a fellow who wants her ladyship, the governor of Hertfordshire, put out of the way. I didn't have anyone to do the job at the time, but now I can take it on after all." He strode to the door. "I'm going out, and under no circumstances are either of you to open any of the doors after I leave." He spoke a few words in Latin.

Susanna recognized it as a lock spell. Uncle Ernie was locking them in?

Neither lady moved or spoke until the front door closed behind Uncle Ernie with a snick of finality. Then, and only then, did Mother turn to look Susanna full in the face.

"Thank heavens he only bespelled the doors and downstairs windows," she said. The return to her usual brisk, practical voice struck Susanna almost as oddly as her uncle's swift alteration to a menacing enemy.

As she spoke, Mother hustled Susanna out of the parlor and up the wide, curving staircase into Ned's old bedroom, where she began to rummage in the chest of drawers. "You must change and escape from here at once. I trust you can climb down the tree?"

"Yes," said Susanna unguardedly. She had done it often enough when she'd been sent to her room for punishment, sneaking out her brother's window to climb into the garden and take his old bicycle for a spin. Sometimes she would watch the antics of the other young people of St. Albans, red-headed Mark Hart at their head, and wish she had courage enough to join them. She never understood why Mother kept them so isolated from the townfolk. "But Mother, why—"

"You must get to Cambridge so Ned can protect you," Mother said, holding up trousers, shirt, and vest. She thrust the clothing at Susanna. "Change, quickly! You must be well on your way before your uncle returns. He will fetch his associates and return before day's end."

Susanna took the clothing helplessly. "I don't understand any of this!"

"You must trust me," Mother said. "Use your wits, if you have any! I cannot tell you any more. Your uncle cursed me when I was a girl. I can only say that if you do not want your magic and your person used against Lady Hart, you must do as I say. Think it out for yourself, but do it while you change."

Susanna obediently began the process of transforming herself into an awkward, gangly boy. When she was fully dressed in her brother's outgrown clothes, Mother picked up a pair of shears.

Susanna's hands flew to her head. "Not my hair!" It was her one claim to beauty: long, thick, and a shining chestnut brown.

The glare Mother gave her silenced this last protest.

Susanna undid her braids with trembling fingers. A real heroine wouldn't cry over losing her hair. To distract herself from the dreadful "click, snip" of the shears, she set her mind to the riddle Mother had set her.

She had heard of spells to compel people to do one's bidding against their own will, but she had always thought them myths. But if not, then not only she but Lady Hart was in grave danger.

Susanna shuddered all over at the thought of losing control of her body, her magic, of becoming nothing more than a pawn for someone else. No wonder Mother had never permitted her or Ned to perform magic in front of Uncle Ernie!

"But surely the governor must have protectors," she said out loud.

Mother's voice behind her head was impatient. "They wouldn't consider a girl a threat. They would guard against a man or even a grown woman, not you. Ernie would—" Her voice stopped.

The scissors clacked against the wooden floorboards as they fell. Susanna turned to look. She saw her mother clutching at her throat, gasping for air.

"Mother!"

Mother waved her back. After another moment of agonized choking, she straightened, taking a few cautious breaths.

"As I was saying," she began, picking the shears back up

and cutting another piece of hair. "Theoretically, *you* could get close enough to cast a spell to injure or even kill her before anyone would notice. You would not escape justice afterward, but—" She stopped, perhaps afraid of the curse.

Susanna could end the sentence well enough on her own. She would be caught but Uncle Ernie would not, and he would curse her as he had her mother so she could not implicate him. Seeing the effects of said curse sparked some fear, but more rage.

"It is wicked!" she burst out.

Not to mention illegal. The entire reason the magical community had governors in place, the reason for the High Council of Magicians, was to ensure things like this didn't happen. Magicians were never to use their powers against other people for ill, and only rarely for good. Too much harm had been done in the past by magicians who wanted to shape the world according to their desires.

Susanna didn't know Lady Hart well. After Father's death, Mother had stopped associating with the other magicians of St. Albans. The governor's reputation was of one who was unyielding but just. Even had she been lazy and corrupt, Susanna still would have rebelled. This sort of magic was more than illegal; it was depraved.

"Which is why you must not let it happen," Mother said. "I finally gave up my magic rather than—than let it keep happening with me."

She finished Susanna's hair, pushed a leather purse into her hand, and turned her to the window.

"Go," she said, and magic or not, her voice had such urgency in it that Susanna swallowed the rest of her questions and went.

Down the tree, accustoming herself to the unusual freedom of trousers rather than long skirts, running swiftly through the garden, out the back gate, and down the road to the train station. She didn't look back.

When she reached the road, she slowed from a run to a leisurely walk, imitating Ned's lanky stride as best she could. Though she'd lived in St. Albans her entire life, nobody recognized her or even gave her a second glance. If she hadn't been so shaken by the morning's events, the sense of freedom would have been delightful.

The usual crowd was at the station, clamoring for tickets to London and beyond. Susanna hesitated a moment before joining the queue inside the office. The train was not the fastest nor the most direct route to Cambridge, but she didn't know how else to get there. She had no horse, no automobile, not even a bicycle.

Her eye rested wistfully on that last item as its owner leaned it casually against the fence before wandering off to watch the trains coming and going.

As the line moved forward, a flash of red hair a few people ahead caught Susanna's eye. What was Lady Hart's son Mark doing here? Surely he had no need to travel by train. Susanna had seen him at the wheel of the Hart automobile, usually with a crowd of young people piled in behind him.

Susanna was sorely tempted to take him aside and confess the entire tale, let him tell his mother and take it out of her hands. She eyed him covertly. He had a reputation of never taking anything seriously. Would he even listen to her? It was a wild story, she had to admit.

No, best to stick with the original plan. Get to Cambridge and Ned.

Besides, she didn't want to be left out of anything. If anyone was going to stop Uncle Ernie, it should be her. She was the one who had started this, so she should be the one ending it.

Forgetting for the moment that she was supposed to be a boy, Susanna tossed her head, garnering some strange looks from the crowd.

Her bravado failed when she caught sight of the uncle in question leaving the queue for the London gate, ticket in hand. Not only did he look far more menacing than she'd ever seen, but he was accompanied by two large men whose air of ruthlessness tainted the space around them. People edged away from the trio without meeting their eyes. Susanna swallowed, suddenly unsure of herself.

She shrank back as Uncle Ernie scanned the line of passengers, inexpressibly relieved when his eye passed over her without recognition. He was here for another purpose, then; he hadn't yet returned to the house to discover her escape. Probably he was leaving to meet his nefarious associates, the ones who wanted Lady Hart assassinated.

Reaching the head of the line, Susanna handed a few coins to the ticket seller.

"One to Cambridge."

This was her chance to prove herself. She would show Mother and Uncle Ernie and everyone that she had what it took to be a serious magician. For once, it was her turn to take care of the people she loved, instead of letting them take care of her.

She pocketed the ticket and slouched against the a nearby wall, waiting until Uncle Ernie was further down the platform before going through the barrier herself. She murmured a spell to alter the appearance of her features. Even if Uncle Ernie got a close look at her, with her boy's clothing and slightly different face, she should be safe. Even if he was taking the train all the way to Cambridge, she could stay one step ahead.

She would use a finding spell on Ned as soon as she reached Cambridge—wearing his clothing was enough of a connection to make such a spell easy—and then the two of them could come back and—

One of the thugs with Uncle Ernie raised his head, as if he were sniffing the air. Then—O horrors!—his gaze narrowed in on Susanna. His lips peeled back from his teeth in a grim smile and started back toward her, pushing through the people waiting for the trains to arrive.

Susanna uttered a word which would have made her mother faint to hear. The man must have been one of the magic-sniffers, as Ned called them, a magician with a special talent for sensing those casting spells in their immediate vicinity.

But there must be other magicians at the station. Why would he notice her in particular?

However it had happened, the result was clear: in trying to cover herself, Susanna had given herself away.

Uncle Ernie turned in the direction his thug was moving. He looked directly at Susanna.

Despite the disguise, his face hardened in recognition. His features convulsed in fury. All three now came toward her, and at this, her nerve broke despite her resolution to be bold and strong.

She shoved back through the barrier and fled the station, the three men hard on her heels. Heads turned to stare at them as they went. Susanna had a moment's fleeting hope that someone would come to her aid, but then her uncle boomed out,

"Stop that boy! He stole my pocketbook!"

Several others joined in the chase.

Thoughts of magic floated through Susanna's mind. But what spell could she do here, in front of so many non-magicians, that would not be noticed? She might escape Uncle Ernie, but she would go down in history as the hysterical girl who betrayed the existence of magic to the rest of England. It was hardly the legacy she dreamed of. Oh, if *only* she had more training!

She darted and wheeled around grasping hands and outstretched arms. "I stole nothing!" she called. "It's all a lie!"

No one heeded her. She was momentarily outraged on behalf of her assumed persona. Really, just because her clothes were somewhat ill-fitting and well-worn and her hair was poorly cropped, there was no reason to automatically take Uncle Ernie's word against hers!

By what she could only consider a miracle, she stumbled out to the road without being caught. One of her well-meaning pursuers darted out almost on her heels, calling for a constable to come and arrest her. She would almost welcome an arrest, since that would prove she hadn't stolen anything, save that Uncle Ernie would find some way to get his talons in her after all.

Knowing him, he would probably pretend sorrow at the mistake and insist on whisking her off to make it up to her, causing all the onlookers to admire his generosity.

Susanna caught sight of the dusty red bicycle still leaning against the fence. Whispering an apology to its owner under her breath, she grabbed the handlebars, flung one leg over hte seat, and started pedaling.

"Stop thief!" cried the police constable, puffing up on foot toward her.

He grabbed at the handlebars, but as his fingers brushed the metal, a red-haired young man crashed into him, knocking him to the ground.

"So sorry!" gasped Mark Hart, landing artistically atop the constable's rounded stomach. He raised his head and looked directly into Susanna's eyes, winking and jerking his head toward the road. She didn't need more of a hint.

She wasn't safe yet. Craning her head over shoulder as she pumped the bicycle into motion, she saw Uncle Ernie slide into the driver's seat of his expensive motor car, the thugs squeezing in behind. She couldn't outrun an automobile on a bicycle.

Luck was with her. No sooner had her uncle pulled onto the road than a farm cart lumbered out in front of him, blocking the way and giving her a chance. It wouldn't be long before Uncle Ernie was after her, but that brief moment was enough to give her a plan.

She steered in the direction of the Ver, the wide, swift-flowing river that separated the town from the old Roman city of Veralamium, and prayed she would reach it before he caught up with her. Susanna put her head down and pedaled for all she was worth.

The motor car was roaring behind her by the time she got to the bridge. No time for second thoughts now: she kicked the bicycle to a stop, grasped the wooden railing, swung herself over, and dropped into the river in one swift motion.

Thank heavens Father had taught her to swim before he

died, improper though many thought it!

Susanna struck out with the current, letting it bolster her efforts to get away. Above and behind her, she heard Uncle Ernie's angry voice.

"After her!"

The grumbles from the thugs indicated neither of them could swim.

"Then cast a spell, you fool!"

O mercy, what was the shield spell Ned had described in his last letter? It was the most complicated spell his tutor had yet taught him, one only meant for those entering a more dangerous area of magical expertise, but like most young men, Ned had taken to it like a duck to water. He described it with precision in his letter, if only Susanna could remember it.

Her memory failed her, but her instincts didn't. As one of the thugs raised his voice in Latin, she had just enough sense to duck wholly under the water and let the current carry her.

Running water hindered magic, and if she couldn't be seen it would be even harder for a spell to affect her.

It seemed to work. At any rate, she didn't feel the shiver of magic connecting to her person.

When she finally had to come up for air, she had drifted a good way downstream. In the distance, she saw Uncle Ernie and his men running down the bank after her. Another moment, and she would be spotted.

Susanna's eyes fell on the willows drooping from the opposite bank to overhang the water.

She kicked out of the current to the other side and sank down beneath the willow branches so that only her eyes and nose were above water. As soon as the three men drew near, she filled her lungs with air and submerged.

When she could hold her breath no longer, she cautiously rose to the surface.

It had worked! They had gone right past her hiding place and were looking for her further down. Susanna waited a few more moments to let them get out of hearing range, and then softly pushed off, making her way upstream.

***

It was twilight by the time the saturated, chilled Susanna crawled out of the stream into a farmer's field. She was too tired to do more than push feebly at the head of the cow that ambled over to sniff at her. Deciding she was not worth stepping on, the cow wandered off again, and Susanna dragged herself to her feet.

What now? Cambridge was out. Uncle Ernie would have guessed she was heading there. Where else would she flee except to Ned?

Maybe it was time to go to Lady Hart, as she had considered earlier. Only ... would Uncle Ernie anticipate that as well? Would he leave a man behind to watch the Hart residence?

No matter what she did, Susanna could be walking into a trap.

She sighed and absently rubbed the nose of the cow who had returned to investigate her further. "I simply don't know what to do," she told it.

"I can tell you what to do," rumbled a voice.

Susanna jumped.

For a heart-stopping moment, she thought the cow had spoken to her. Then a man stepped out from the shadows of the trees lining the field and she realized the truth.

It was Uncle Ernie's magic-finder.

"How did you find me?"

He smirked at her dismay. "You never ended your little spell back at the station. When we lost you downstream, all I had to do was backtrack and sniff around until I picked it up again."

Susanna gaped. What a colossally stupid mistake! How could she have been so foolish?

"*Finiatur,*" she murmured, and felt the snap as the spell closed.

The main reason for never allowing a spell to continue indefinitely rushed in on her as her knees grew weak and her vision blurred. Sustaining magic for that long sapped one's strength and energy, and ending it abruptly brought a nasty backlash.

She tried to hold herself upright, but the effort was too much, and the field and sky grew black around her as she crashed to the ground. The cow's incurious, "mooo," was the last thing she heard.

***

Susanna came to with a gasp. What had happened?

It all rushed in on her—losing her temper, Uncle Ernie's diabolical scheme, Mother's plan, rushing off to Ned, the river, and then getting captured at the last. None of it seemed possible, yet here she was.

It was too dark to see where "here" was. Her hands and feet were bound. She was sitting against a rough wall; it scratched her back even through her vest and shirt. Judging by the wall and the odors that floated past her nose, she was in a barn.

Susanna groaned. What a mess she'd made of everything!

"Thank goodness you're awake."

Susanna gave a strangled shriek. "Who's there?"

"Are you all right? How's your head? Your first time overstepping your strength as a magician? The first time is always the worst."

"Who *are* you?" Susanna demanded in response to this spate of questions. "What are you doing here?"

"Mark Hart," her companion said.

Susanna was thankful for the darkness as she gaped.

He continued, "I can't work magic myself, but I can tell when someone is using it."

"You too?"

"It's not as exciting as it sounds, I promise. I noticed you at the station. I thought it odd that your magic had the same feel to it as that scoundrel Ernest Lawton's, when I knew his nephew was away at university—"

More shocks. "You know Uncle Ernie? You know who my brother is? What do you mean, my magic feels like his?"

"My mother's been keeping an eye on your uncle for magical infractions for years, though she's never been able to pin anything on him. So I know a bit about your family. Nothing much, just who you are. But magic-users from the same family often have a similar feel to their spellwork."

Susanna groaned again. So that was how the other magic-sniffer had picked her out of the crowd.

"I could tell you were trying to get away from Lawton, so I figured I'd help. Once I realized you were, you know, *you*, the niece, I was intrigued. I followed the trace of your spell down the river, and I tried to stop that fellow from taking you, but I—well, he overpowered me. Sorry."

"Don't apologize!" To her horror, Susanna found tears filling her eyes. It had been a long time since anyone had gone out of his or her way to help her. She cleared her throat. "I am most grateful for your attempt," she said primly.

She could hear the smile in Mark's voice. "Then in recompense, do you mind telling me what I've landed in?"

She told him the entire story, from that morning's defiance to the moment she crawled out of the river.

"And I've made an awful mess of it," she ended mournfully. "I think my mother was right; I'm not cut out to be a magician. I couldn't even think of a spell to combat Uncle Ernie and his men. My magic betrayed me at the start, was useless for the entire chase, and then betrayed me again at the end. I would have been better off not using it at all."

"As for that, I'd rather have sharp wits and no magic at all than the finest arsenal of spells and not an ounce of common sense," Mark said. "I can't use magic at all, but somehow I manage to jog along."

Susanna couldn't think what to say to that. Thankfully, he didn't wait for a response.

"Now that we've got that settled, let's both of us use our wits to get out of here and save my mother. Are you recovered enough to give us some light?"

"Certainly," Susanna said. She had no idea whether she really was or not, but after what he'd said about magic and wits she would give them light or die trying. "*Lux fiat.*"

A green ball of light sprang to life above her head, illuminating the room in which they sat.

As she had deduced, they were in a barn. No animals or guards, nothing save herself, her fellow prisoner, and a lone pitchfork. She turned her head to look properly at Mark. His hair gleamed a sickly bronze in the light, his left eye was badly bruised, his lip was cut, but he grinned encouragingly at her.

"Nicely done!"

Despite everything, Susanna grinned back. She spoke the words to untie their hands and feet. Free at last, she spent a few moments rubbing life back into her stiff limbs.

"Can you sense any traps?" she asked.

He frowned, looking around. "No—not exactly. They've done magic here, but I can't tell what. My senses must be a little shaken up after my quarrel with that bruiser."

Susanna's rush of admiration was mixed with guilt. He had received those bruises and injuries in trying to help her.

Putting that out of her mind for the moment, she focused on the matter at hand. It didn't make any sense, no guards and no traps. Did her uncle think so poorly of her, and of Mark, that he wouldn't bother guarding against their escape?

She grabbed the pitchfork and walked over to the large double doors leading outside. Standing well back against the wall, with Mark a step behind, she ended her light spell and eased the closest door open.

She blinked against the rush of moonlight and fresh air flooding into the barn. Freedom! They would escape the barn and then ... she grinned mercilessly. Uncle Ernie would be in for a surprise.

Still holding the pitchfork, just in case, Susanna set her foot on the threshold of the barn. She bounced backward as though from hitting a wall.

She shook her head and tentatively put out her free hand. It stopped, pushed back invisibly in midair. No matter how hard she pushed, she couldn't go through.

"Of course they wouldn't leave us unprotected," Mark

said, voice laced with disgust. "They set up a ward. Dormant until someone tried to go through, so I wouldn't sense it clearly. Sneaky."

"It's a safe guess they attached a warning device to it, to let them know when it activated," Susanna said. "They're probably on their way here right now."

Mark looked grim. "Better let me have the pitchfork. When they get here, I'll hold them off long enough for you to escape."

"Rubbish!" Susanna said, forgetting for a moment to whom she was speaking. "As if I'd leave you behind. I have a better plan."

Mark narrowed his eyes. "Really?"

She didn't, but something teased at the back of her mind from this morning—only this morning!—with Mother. Uncle Ernie had warded the doors but not the upstairs windows. There was a chance he had learned from his mistake, but on the other hand, he was arrogant enough that perhaps he hadn't.

"Wait here!" she cried.

In a flash, Susanna climbed the ladder to the haymow and tested the small window. It wasn't large enough for a full-grown man to fit through, and it led out onto empty air. It wasn't so surprising that Uncle Ernie had indeed neglected to block it.

Susanna peered over the edge of the haymow at Mark. "Do you think you can fit through here?" she asked.

Mark grinned. "Just try me." He held out a hand to help her back down the ladder. "I think I'm going to like this plan."

Back on the mail floor, Susanna collected the ropes that

had bound them and handed them to Mark, who knotted them together and carried them up to the haymow, tying one end around the beam closest to the window.

While he did that, Susanna set the pitchfork against the wall where she had been propped earlier. She wove a glamour around it, making the simple farm implement look like a girl with short, ragged hair, dressed in her brother's clothes.

There was nothing she could use to set up an image of Mark, but in the dim light coming from the open door, she hoped this would be enough.

The scene set, Mark climbed out the window first, testing to make sure the rope would hold. Susanna followed, finding the climb somewhat trickier than she'd anticipated. Her arms gave out at the same time the rope ended, and she dropped the final few feet.

Mark caught her and set her on the ground. "Now what?"

"This."

Susanna closed her mind to her scrapes and fatigue as she laid a hand on the barn wall.

Setting a full ward was beyond her skill, she could admit that now. Mark had taken away the shame she felt in her paltry abilities. Altering someone else's ward, though ... that wasn't all that different from any of those small household magics Uncle Ernie had sneered at that morning.

Susanna concentrated. An outline of the spell appeared in her mind, and she was able to change its parameters with a few words.

"*Finiatur*," she ended, closing her mouth with a snap. She wasn't going to be caught leaving a spell active again!

The end was almost tame after that. Uncle Ernie roared up in his motor car. He and his men passed through the ward, lured in by the image of Susanna still helplessly tied against the wall.

Several long, excruciating moments passed before the sound of angry shouts and thumps indicated the men had tried to walk back out and failed.

"Ha!" Mark yelped. Susanna laughed as he picked her up and spun her around. "Fancy a spin in your uncle's motor car?"

Mark drove them to the Hart residence, where Lady Hart met them, stately even in a dressing gown and slippers. She sent people to collect Ernie and his thugs and sat the two of them down for the complete tale.

At the end of it, she contemplated Susanna.

"You are entirely self-taught, Miss Westwood?"

"Through my brother's letters," Susanna said, giving credit where it was due.

"Impressive. Resourceful. Your age?"

"Seventeen today, my lady." Susanna laughed in surprise. "I had forgotten!"

Lady Hart ignored this digression. "I shall give you tomorrow to recover from your adventures, Miss Westwood, and then I expect you to present yourself back here. I shall take charge of your education myself."

She swept out of the room before Susanna could muster a response.

Mark grinned at her flabbergasted face.

"Many happy returns of the day, Susanna," he said.

Passion &

Practicality

A piercing scream rang through the stone cottage, penetrating even the sound-muffling spell Evelyn had set up around her workroom.

She started, dropping the beaker holding the wart-removal potion she had spent the last hour painstakingly concocting. Evelyn tightened her lips in annoyance.

"What now, Violet?" she muttered under her breath.

Her older sister's histrionics got worse every year. Evelyn kept hoping eventually Violet would learn to practice moderation, but it seemed increasingly unlikely.

Evelyn mopped up the spilled potion with a linen rag, tossed it into the pail of special cleaning solution she kept ready at all times for magical spills, and glided downstairs to see what had caused Violet's shriek this time.

She descended the last step to see her sister in the front hall, wild-eyed and with her dark curls in riotous disorder, standing over the prone body of a man lying just inside the open door.

"Oh Evie, I think I killed him," Violet gasped, and burst into tears.

Evelyn whisked past, dropping a handkerchief into her sister's outstretched hand as she went, and knelt carefully in her long wool skirt beside the man. She reached a careful hand to pick up his limp arm, shuddering slightly at the lack of resistance. She pressed two fingers against the inside of his wrist the way Dr. Harris had done when Mama died, feeling for a pulse.

After a couple moments, she let it drop and stood up, wiping her hands fastidiously against her skirt, wishing she could wash them properly.

"He is most certainly dead, Vi."

Violet's only response to this was to sob more loudly into the handkerchief.

"Do calm down and explain," Evelyn said.

Vi's deep blue eyes peered at her above the top of the dainty lawn square. "Calm down? Calm down! How can I calm down when I have become a murderess?"

Evelyn wondered if a cup of tea would help. Looking at Violet's shaking shoulders, she regretfully decided probably not unless she first laced it with brandy.

"Did he attack you?" she asked.

"I did not give him the chance," Violet said. "I came into the hall to find him standing here, with the door open, a stranger in our house!" She drew herself up, tears forgotten. "I demanded to know who he was and what he was doing. Instead of answering, he started toward me with the most horrific leer on his face. I was terrified, naturally, but instead of running away or fainting uselessly, I defended our house."

Meaning she had lost her head and released a self-defense spell which, fueled by her panic and lack of self control, was too powerful and killed instead of stunning.

Nevertheless, it was self-defense, not murder, and the man was an intruder in their home.

"Most distressing indeed, Vi, but I do not think you need fret overly much," Evelyn said. "We shall simply tell Domestic Protection what happened and—"

She got no further.

Violet released a heart-rending scream, even louder than the one which had brought Evelyn from her workroom. "You would turn your own sister over to the unfeeling brutes of Domestic Protection? After I protected us—protected you, hidden away in your little room, unaware of the danger lurking below! I did not believe even you could be so cruel. Why not call the police and have me arrested as a common criminal instead?"

Evelyn ignored this last suggestion.

"What would you have me do, Vi? Hide the corpse and pretend nothing happened?" In her exasperation, Evelyn did not measure her words as carefully as was her wont. In her defense, this had been a particularly trying day.

Violet brightened at once. "Oh Evie, you are so clever! I knew you wouldn't leave me in such dire straits."

"Violet, we are not—" Evelyn began, when what promised to be a rousing argument was interrupted by a smart "rat-a-tat-rap" on the door knocker.

Evelyn swallowed her words while Violet hastily cast the *Advena Cognosco* spell to see who was at the door. The sisters stared at each other in dismay when the small image of Amelia Rawlings appeared in the air before them.

Miss Amelia Rawlings, spinster and ambitious magician, was the worst gossip in Hertfordshire. Informing the local branch of magical authorities of Violet's mishap was one thing. Allowing Amelia to get a hold of it was another entirely.

"Right," said Evelyn.

Levitating a human body was beyond her skills. Levitating a rag rug upon which a dead body reposed, she now learned, was not.

She hastily directed the rug with its macabre load into the kitchen, thanking the stars it was the maid-of-all-work's day off. Minnie was a good soul, but she would not have responded favorably to a corpse on the kitchen table.

Evelyn closed the kitchen door while Violet pinched color back into her cheeks, dried her teary eyes, and fixed a smile on her face. Armor in position, the two exchanged a quick nod, and Violet opened the front door.

Petite and fashionably rounded, Amelia Rawlings was always garbed in the latest fashions from Paris. Today she was in a long silvery-green skirt and matching jacket with a white ermine collar that even under these circumstances made Violet's eyes gleam with envy. The jacket was artfully cut so as to show the rows of purple ruffles cascading down her silk shirtwaist. A green hat with purple and yellow plumes perched atop her blonde hair completed the *ensemble*.

Style, power, wealth, and an insatiable nose for gossip. It was no wonder most people disliked Amelia Rawlings. The only area in which she did not excel was that of finding a husband, being now thirty years of age and still single.

Since Violet had attained that same age without a husband, and Evelyn was close behind, they couldn't even reassure themselves of their superiority in that area.

"Good afternoon, ladies!" Amelia said, her eyes gleaming with their usual bird-like alertness. "What a time you took coming to the door! Is everything in order here? Any troubles?"

"Good afternoon, Amelia, do come in," said Violet.

Evelyn conceded that her sister's dramatic tendencies were occasionally of use. Her performance rivaled that of Mrs. Siddons. Not even Amelia Rawlings could shake her apparent poise.

"You mustn't jump to such dreadful conclusions," Vi continued with a light laugh as Evelyn took Amelia's outerwear and parasol. "It's Minnie's day out, that's all, and both Evelyn and I were engaged in spellwork when you rang. You of all people should appreciate taking the time to properly end a spell rather than leaving it running while we scamper off to greet a guest!"

"Ah."

Amelia seemed disappointed, but quickly recovered. "Have you two heard the latest news? Evelyn, bring tea into the parlor and I'll tell you both all about it."

Evelyn smothered her irritation at being given orders by a guest in her own house. Getting annoyed at Amelia was the same thing as getting annoyed at Vi—the only person who felt her irritation was her.

Making tea was not the soothing occupation it normally was, with a dead body resting on the table top. While the water boiled, Evelyn steeled herself to examine him—it—further, hoping to find some evidence of who he was, why he was here, and what was behind all this.

Her search, performed with extreme distaste, revealed only that the man had no identification, not even a monogrammed handkerchief, on him. This in itself was striking.

Someone deliberately concealing his identity? But why?

The kettle boiled, and Evelyn had to shelve the problem long enough to be a proper hostess.

She carried the tray of tea and store-bought biscuits into the parlor, where Vi and Amelia sat making small talk.

"At last, what an age you've been," said Amelia, who surely never ventured into her own kitchen for any reason but to give her cook orders. "Come, sit, I *must* tell you my news before I burst."

Tea poured and biscuits distributed—Amelia sniffed over

the fact that they weren't homemade but took four all the same—the sisters finally heard Amelia's tale.

"I was visiting Anne Spencer yesterday, and she told me her cousin Alexander is returning from India for a visit! He should be here any day, possibly even today."

Vi's face paled. Evelyn wanted to reach for her hand, but did not dare under Amelia's all-seeing eye.

"I knew the news would shock you, Violet dear, so I thought it best if I told you first. It's been what, ten years since he jilted you?"

Violet raised her chin. "Eight, and there was no jilting. It was a childish infatuation, a boy-and-girl romance, and it died —" Her voice caught in her throat as her eyes filled with horror.

Evelyn knew at once where her sister's thoughts had gone.

It had been eight years since they had last seen Alexander Spencer, though as both he and Vi were twenty-two at the time it was hardly the youthful romance Vi made it out to be. Eight years was a long time for anyone. Might Alex have grown into the man now lying dead on their kitchen table? Could he have rushed to visit his old sweetheart upon his return home from India, not bothering to knock, never thinking she wouldn't know him at once? Could Violet, in her panic, have mistaken a joyful smile and rush to embrace her for a leer and threatening movement?

It was all too plausible.

Evelyn prided herself on her clear-headedness and logical mind, and these pieces fit together in an unhappily likely pattern.

After all, who else could it be? A burglar? There had been reports of a gang of robbers in the area. But then, there were always those sorts of dramatic rumors floating around that never came to anything, and besides, burglars didn't come in the front door in the middle of the day.

An enemy? Nonsense. Evelyn blushed just thinking along such melodramatic lines.

Luckily, Amelia mistook Vi's reaction for one of extreme anxiety at the thought of meeting Alexander Spencer again. She smirked, clearly pleased to have gotten this reaction.

"Well, I'll leave you two to your spellwork," she said, rising to her feet.

She no doubt wanted to spread the news of Vi's reaction around town, Evelyn thought bitterly. As if they hadn't enough to endure without that!

"Goodbye, Amelia," she said, escorting her to the door.

Amelia chattered some more about that same gang of robbers Evelyn had heard of, how Anne was thankful to have a man around for protection from them, and weren't Evelyn and Violet worried, out here all on their own?

Evelyn could barely keep from laughing in her face.

She finally got the gossipy magician out the door and immediately rushed back to Vi, who sat in the exact same position she had been in since Amelia dropped the news.

"It's him—it was him—it was Alex, come to make up our quarrel, returned to me at last—and I killed him!"

She burst into sobs interspersed with shrieks of wild laughter. Evelyn recognized the signs of hysteria. She administered a soothing potion and put Violet to bed before returning to the kitchen to face what must be done.

Clearly, she could not leave Vi to face the consequences of her actions. Even before the recognition of the dead man, Violet was in no position to take responsibility for what she'd done. This revelation only made it more impossible. Evelyn had to do it for her.

The entire reason Evelyn had refused to marry Henry Talbot seven years ago was because she had promised her mother to always look after and protect Violet.

"I know it's unfair," her mother had whispered, pale and sweating with the fever. "She's the elder, she's supposed to take care of you. But you're the sensible one, my Evie. She needs your steadfastness to hold firm. Promise me you'll never abandon her."

Evelyn had so promised, and she had held to it even when her heart yearned for a new life and the love of a good man. But after the quarrel with and subsequent separation from Alex, Vi had been in far too emotionally fragile a state to see her sister happily married. Nor could she have endured living as a spinster sister-in-law in Henry's house.

Now again, Evelyn had to make whatever sacrifice was necessary to take care of Vi.

She couldn't leave a dead body on her kitchen table, nor could she bury it in the back garden. If it was Alex Spencer— and Evelyn accepted Violet's identification—his family deserved to know he was dead.

That left her with really only one choice. She couldn't drag the body outside somewhere for a stranger to find and report to Domestic Protection. The residue from Vi's spell lingered, and it was possible Deep had acquired a Finer—a magician who could trace spells back to their casters.

The only thing left to do was a misdirection. And the only person to misdirect Deep's attention toward ... was herself.

Half an hour later, her preparations complete, Evelyn

braced herself and summoned Henry Talbot.

He didn't respond at once. Of course, Henry would never lower himself to rush to answer her call!

Evelyn bit her lip, wondering if she should contact someone else. But she didn't know anyone else at Deep, and she shrank from exposing this affair to strangers. Eventually the news would get out to all, but not yet; she would postpone that evil moment as long as possible.

Even Henry's scorn was to be preferred to the gossip, speculation, pity—especially the pity—of strangers.

Finally, the water in the scrying bowl trembled. Evelyn set the silver bowl on the scrying table after checking to make sure Violet was still asleep.

Henry's face, plain, strong, and stubborn, still as familiar as her own after all these years, appeared in the bowl.

"Evelyn?"

His voice was flattened slightly by the spell, but it still quickened her pulse.

"I wish to report a crime," she said, trying to keep her voice steady. "Or an accident."

He frowned. How well she knew that expression!

"Which is it, Evelyn? Kindly be precise."

"I would be if I could," she snapped, immediately regretting it. Only Henry had the ability to make her lose self-control like that. "Something has occurred—I have done something—I cannot explain it like this. I must show you."

His eyebrows lifted. She had always loathed that supercilious expression. He did it so well.

"We are rather busy at Deep right now, Evelyn. I can't just up and leave on your say-so. You must give me a little more than that."

"I am not asking you over for a social call," Evelyn said, losing her temper thoroughly over the insinuation she was wasting his time—and possibly chasing after him. "I have killed Alexander Spencer, if you must hear it over so public a channel. I did not intend to, but it is done, and done by my hand. Is that important enough to take you away from your important schedule, or should I leave his body to rot?"

She stopped, furious now at herself as much as Henry. She should have reported this to a stranger after all, no matter the revulsion to her finer feelings.

"Evelyn." Henry stopped and began again. "Is this true?"

Evelyn stared coldly into the scrying bowl. "I have never lied to you, Henry."

She cut the spell, her stomach souring as she realized that statement, now, was itself a lie.

She sank to the floor in a rustle of skirts and petticoats, allowing two tears to course down her cheeks before she regained control.

She would do whatever it took to save Vi—but at the moment she hated herself, and almost hated her sister, for so doing.

A knock thundering against the front door interrupted her self-pity. Evelyn didn't need a spell to tell it was Henry. He must have used magic to get himself here from the local Deep station so quickly.

Evelyn walled her emotions away and rose to answer the knock.

Pacing impatiently on the doorstep, Henry appeared as disheveled as she'd ever seen him. He had come out without overcoat or hat, his fair hair rumpled and his coat unbuttoned. Even his tie, a sober navy blue color, had tilted askew.

He grabbed her arms with unconsciously bruising force. "Evelyn! Are you hurt?"

She put her hands on his chest and pushed him away. "I am uninjured, Henry, though my arms are now slightly sore."

He dropped his hands at once.

"I suppose you want to see the body?" she continued. "It is in the kitchen."

"In the kitchen—never mind that!" He reached for her again, then forced himself to pull his arms back. "For heaven's sake, tell me what happened!"

She recited her prepared story mechanically. She knew she was making a bad job of it, but seeing Henry in person had badly jolted her. Aside from his general air of untidiness, he hadn't changed a bit in seven years.

Her tongue felt thick in her mouth as she spoke.

"I was in the kitchen making scones for tea when I sensed someone behind me. I was already on edge—we'd heard peculiar noises all through the night and I was aware of rumors of burglars in the neighborhood. You know you always said it wasn't safe for two women to live alone. I spun around with a hastily prepared defense spell at the ready, and as soon as I saw the strange man behind me, I panicked and let fly. It was stronger than I'd intended, and it hit his heart and killed him."

It would have been simpler to move the body back into the hall and tell the story exactly as it had occurred, with her in place of Violet. But Henry would never have believed it.

Evelyn could just barely picture herself panicking if she was surprised while she was at work in the kitchen, back to an intruder. But she would never have done so coming upon a stranger in the front hall, even if he approached her. Given even the smallest amount of warning, she would have controlled the spell enough to have to exactly as she wished and no more.

If she couldn't see it happening that way, Henry certainly wouldn't. She had to make this improbable deed seem at least possible.

Henry's face gradually froze into its typical stone-like expression as she continued. She couldn't tell what he was thinking.

"Then Violet appeared in the doorway and screamed. She recognized him at once as Alex Spencer. He had returned from overseas and come to visit her, entering by way of the kitchen because that's what he'd always done when they were children, so he could wheedle goodies from Minnie. I got Violet calmed down as best I could and put her to bed, and immediately contacted you. I did not intend to kill him, but I did." She finished off with a small sigh, feeling unutterably tired now that was all out. "I suppose you have to arrest me now?"

Henry's expression was still frozen. "First I'd like to see the body," he said. "You may stay here if you wish."

"No," said Evelyn. "I'll show you. I can't shy away from my responsibility, can I?"

"You never could," he agreed wryly, standing aside to led her lead the way.

She had arranged the body artistically right before the door leading to the back garden, still on the rug as she couldn't easily pull it out from underneath. She longed to burn it, but that would have to be left to Violet after Henry took her, Evelyn, away.

Henry stopped short as soon as he saw the scene. "There really is a body," he said softly.

"Of course there is," Evelyn said, a bite to her words. "Did you think I made it all up?"

He shook his head. "No. I just ... I don't know, Evelyn. I don't think I quite took it in before."

She relented. "It is quite fantastic," she conceded.

He took a step closer to the body. A frown marred his profile. "Are you certain this is Alexander Spencer?"

"Of course," she said sadly. "Vi recognized him."

"It's been eight years."

"Would you forget?"

His eyes held hers a moment. "No."

Evelyn found her breath coming more quickly. "Well then."

He turned back to the corpse. "It makes sense, but still ... I would have expected finer clothing." He wriggled his shoulders in his characteristic fashion, dismissing it. He held his hands over the body, muttering a finding spell.

Evelyn schooled her face to show none of her emotions, forcing even her fingers to be still. This was the test.

A true Finder would be able to tell there were two spells on the body, hers layered over Violet's. It was another reason she had contacted Henry—he was weak in Finding, and she had counted on him coming out alone at first. By the time they had a proper Finder here to confirm the magical nature of the man's death, Vi's spell residue would have faded, leaving only Evelyn's signature.

Henry waited a few moments, then sighed. "Killed by a defensive spell all right," he said. "And it bears your mark."

He turned away from both Evelyn and the body, staring

instead at the wall. "I have to report this, you know. I cannot protect you."

Evelyn was surprised the thought had even occurred to him. It hadn't to her.

"I know, Henry. I know you'd never turn aside from your duty. I did wrong, and I am prepared to accept the consequences."

Henry swore, tugged violently at the back of his collar, and spun back around to face her.

"How can you talk like that, Evelyn? Don't you know what you are doing to me? Did you ask me here to punish me for what happened seven years ago? How can I choose between my duty and the woman I—I once wanted to marry?"

"What I am doing to you? Since when is this about you, Henry? Oh, of course—everything is about you, things only become important as they relate to you. Have you thought for a moment what this is doing to me? I killed a man, a man I respected and liked and for whom my sister cared deeply, and not only do I have to live with that burden for the rest of my life, I had to bring the man I once hoped to marry back into my life to officially report it because he is the only one I can trust to not jump to conclusions about the event!"

They stayed staring at each other for a long, fraught moment.

Then Henry took two long steps forward, caught Evelyn's chin in one hand and encircled her waist with the other, and kissed her.

She could have pulled away if she wanted—his grip was firm but not confining—but she did not move.

"Right," he said at last, stepping back. "That's that."

Evelyn, for once, couldn't think of a single thing to say.

Henry slipped his hand from her waist to entwine his fingers with hers. Clasping her to his side, he surveyed the room once again, this time with narrowed eyes and pursed lips. Evelyn dazedly wondered when this nightmare had turned to a dream and when it was going to shift back. That it would shift was inevitable. People didn't get to be as happy as she was this moment without a price to pay for it.

Then Henry laughed. "Of course. I should have known. You're martyring yourself again, aren't you, my dear fool of a girl?"

Evelyn cleared her throat. She knew she ought to pull her hand away, but she couldn't quite make herself. "I don't know what you're talking about, and while I may very well be a fool, I have not been a girl for many a long season."

"You were not making scones when an intruder entered, this man did not die in the kitchen, and I'm starting to doubt he's Alexander Spencer at all."

"Again, you are calling me a liar!" Evelyn cried.

This time she did tug her hand free, and at the same time stepped further away from Henry. It was too disconcerting being close to him. She hoped her indignation sounded natural.

"You cleverly scattered flour across the table and set a bowl on it to make it appear you were making scones," Henry said. "But if you had been working with dough and spun around to cast a spell, flour would have scattered across the floor from your outstretched arms."

He was right. She had missed that detail.

Bother the man, and she'd been so proud of her foresight in setting the yellow scone dough bowl on the table and artistically sprinkling flour around it.

"Also, I recognize that hideously ugly rug, it belongs in the front hall."

"We moved it," Evelyn countered. "Because it's ugly."

Henry shook his head. "If you had moved it, you would have replaced it with a new rug—well, you might not, because you are so frugal, but Violet certainly would never leave the front hall floor bare. Which it is, because I noticed that when I came in. Besides, who would put a rug there, by the garden door? It would interfere with opening and closing the door and constantly get bunched. No, the only true thing in this entire scene is the dead man, and the only reason you would go to so much trouble to concoct this elaborate story is to protect Violet. Why don't you tell me the truth?"

Evelyn pinched her lips together and refused to rise to the bait. She should have risked the Finder! Henry was too clever and observant by half. She could never equal his cunning—though she defied anyone to say her brains were less than his.

"No?" he said. "Then let me try to reconstruct it. Violet accidentally killed this man, most likely in the front hall so that he landed on the rug, and rather than let her take responsibility for her own actions for once in her life, you stepped in as usual to rescue her. You moved him in here, set the scene, and called upon me, hoping I'd still be so angry over your refusal to marry me seven years ago that I wouldn't look too closely at what really happened. Oh yes, and you must have cast a second self-defense spell over Violet's—I'm assuming that's what did it for this poor chap—so I would only find yours and not sense hers. The only thing I'm not certain of is why you insisted he was Alexander Spencer?"

"He is," Evelyn said, ignoring the rest of it. "Violet said so."

Henry eyed her shrewdly. "Did Violet see him beyond the moment she killed him?"

"You mean the moment after I killed him" Evelyn said. "No."

"Then I must doubt her identification. Look, Evie."

Evelyn's heart flipped at this use of her nickname. She reminded herself that Vi needed her to stay strong.

"The coloring matches Alex's, yes, and he is the same general height and build, but other than that, does he look anything like the Alex you remember? Even allowing for eight years in the Indian climate. Look at the heaviness of his jowls, the cruelty lines marking his mouth and eyes! Can you imagine our Alex developing those sort of lines? Alex, who was the kindest, jolliest soul in the world? Look at his nose, red and bulbous, the sign of too much drink. Alex had far too much self-respect to turn into a drunkard. And just look at the cut of his clothes, the material of them and the way they are made! Could Alex ever bring himself to wear such shoddy work, especially if he was coming to visit Vi after all these years? No, no. Stop thinking with your fears and use your head, darling fool."

A weight lifted off Evelyn's shoulders. Henry was right—he had to be—it was one of his more annoying traits, that he was never wrong.

If that was so, then Alex Spencer was still alive, and Vi did not have to live with the knowledge that she had destroyed the man she loved.

"Who do you think he is, then?" she asked. "And I do not admit the rest of your deductions. We like having the rug in front of the back door because it keeps out drafts, Vi has been meaning to replace it in the front hall but hasn't had time, and I cleaned up the flour on the floor while I waited for you to answer my summons. But allowing you to be correct on this one point, who is he?"

Henry shook his head, but did not press the matter. "That is the question, is it not? Had he been killed in the front hall rather than here in the kitchen, I might have had an answer for you, but as you insist he died here, I am at a loss."

Evelyn glared at him. He stared back with his most irritating smile.

"It doesn't matter who," she said at last, determined not to give an inch. "He is still dead, and that at my hand. You are going to have to arrest me, Henry. Is it manslaughter when it was unintentional?"

"At worst, it would be an improper use of a defensive spell," he said. "No imprisonment necessary, merely a fine and, depending on the severity of the offense, a six month to five year block put on your magical abilities. My dear girl, did you think we would put you in a common jail with hardened criminals?"

"Oh."

Evelyn couldn't help but feel deflated. All that working herself up, lying and sacrificing herself to save Violet, and it was nothing more than a slap on the wrist. Given Violet's clean record and the fact that this man was an intruder rather than an impetuous gentleman caller, she likely would have gotten the minimum sentence.

A magic block was frustrating and publicly humiliating, but nothing worse. It was overseen by trained Deep specialists and actually implemented by the magician herself, a voluntary walling off of that extra sense that gave magicians their ability to manipulate the natural world.

Still, the humiliation alone would be enough to destroy Violet. What would people like Amelia Rawlings say!

They would say it about Evelyn, too, but she cared far less about public opinion than her sensitive sister. Her act was perhaps not as heroic as she had initially thought, but it was no less necessary.

Besides, she wouldn't give Henry the opportunity to gloat over being right.

"Then that is what I shall accept," she said.

His patronizing, amused smile changed abruptly to a scowl. "Evelyn, when will you ever see sense? When will you realize that this incessant over-protection of your sister is doing neither of you any favors? At some point she has to take responsibility for her own life, and equally so you must release your cherished delusion that you are indispensable to her well-being!"

"I recall you making the same argument seven years ago when you tried to persuade me to marry you and leave her all alone," Evelyn shot back. "It seems to me that your lofty ideals have a strong motivation of selfishness behind them. You would have me break my promise to my dying mother for your own ease. You only want me to abandon Vi so you can claim my attention for yourself."

"I vow, if you ever tried to coddle and shield me the way you do your sister, I would ..." He trailed off, apparently unable to think of a dire enough threat.

"Throw me out into the streets to fend for myself?" she suggested.

"I would give you half a dozen children to claim and divide your attention," he said instead, ignoring her sarcasm. "With that many demands on your protectiveness, you would have to learn to let people grow up and stand on their own two feet or else you would simply die of exhaustion."

"How charming of you to put it that way."

"If you weren't such a ridiculous, infuriating woman, I—"

"You what?" she inquired, eyes snapping dangerously.

Henry raised his hands then dropped them, the fire going out of him. "I never would have fallen in love with you," he ended ruefully. "Dash it, Evie, what am I going to do with you?"

"I am not asking you to 'do' anything with me," she fired back, not one whit softened by his capitulation. "I am my own woman, capable of making my own decisions for good or for ill, and you have neither the right nor the authority to tell me what to do."

"No," he said softly. "And neither do you for your sister."

***

That evening, Evelyn had the chance to reflect further on Henry's words. She remained obdurate against all his persuasion, and he had finally been left with no choice but to make an official report and turn her over to the authorities.

Violet had slept through the entire thing. Evelyn had perhaps given her too large a dose of the soothing potion or, more likely, she had been overcome by the violence of her emotions. Evelyn had left her a note stating that the dead man was not Alexander Spencer and that she was being taken to Domestic Protection to face the consequences for killing him.

She trusted Vi would understand what Evelyn had done without needing further explanation.

Henry's colleagues were gruff but kind enough in their

own way. An older woman with her grey hair pulled back in a severe bun and spectacles perched on the end of her long nose took Evelyn's statement and escorted her to a small room in the drab house on the outskirts of town Deep used for their station. There Evelyn would stay while they discussed the case and determined the severity of her sentence.

Left with nothing to do but think, Evelyn was faced with some uncomfortable truths.

One was that no matter how he infuriated her, she still loved Henry. That she put aside to think more on later.

The comments he had made about her relationship with Vi rankled. Was she doing to her sister the very thing she loathed when Henry did it to her?

Deciding what was best for another person and forcing one's own principles and opinions on that person was atrocious, regardless of who was doing it to whom. She at least could argue with Henry when he started high-handedly laying down the law to her. Did anything stop her from charging full strength over Vi?

Evelyn admitted she was prone to believing herself the downtrodden one. She had unconsciously constructed a narrative in her head of herself as the noble, selfless sister, sacrificing everything she might ever have wanted for her sister's sake. It was an uncomfortable thought that perhaps her selflessness was a form of oppression, her sacrifices of form of enslavement for Vi.

Evelyn looked back on the last ten years of life—ever since their parents died one after the other in the dreadful flu epidemic that spring—in a new light. She squirmed inwardly at the way she now saw things: Violet kept repressed until she could only break out via overly dramatic episodes; herself as domineering and cold, refusing even love in order to keep her position of power over her sister.

In a way, she was guilty of murder after all, if not the one she had accused herself of. She was guilty of killing the woman Vi might have become, as well as the woman Evelyn herself could have been had she not poured her grief over her parents' deaths into an iron determination she would never again lose the person she cared most about.

Her promise to her mother, made in a spasm of grief, had warped into something beyond what that good soul could have intended.

No wonder Henry despised her. At that moment, Evelyn despised herself.

The door to her small room opened.

"*Lux fiat*," a dry voice said.

Evelyn blinked as a blueish light burst to life above her head, illuminating the grey-haired Deep woman who had cast the spell.

"Have they come to a decision?" Evelyn asked, keeping her voice steady with an effort.

The woman nodded. "Will you please come downstairs?" she asked.

Evelyn followed her down the winding stairs into the well lit front room, the cold blue light hovering above their heads filling her soul with dread.

In the front room, Henry awaited her alone. The grey-haired woman escorted her in, then retreated along with her light, closing the door behind her.

"What is it, Henry?" Evelyn asked.

He regarded her unblinkingly. Then he stepped to one side, revealing another door behind him. This he opened and

Violet and—Evelyn was unable to believe her eyes at first—Alexander Spencer stepped through.

It was unquestionably Alex. Evelyn wondered how she and Vi could ever have mistaken another man for him. He was suaver, skin darkened by the Indian sun, more polished and confident, but still the same Alex they had always known.

Violet herself was another surprise. As poised as Evelyn had ever seen her without it being an act, a new quiet dignity about her, her arm tucked into the crook of Alex's elbow, Violet seemed to have poured all the growing-up she'd denied herself—or Evelyn had denied her—into the course of a few hours.

"You are free to go, Evelyn," Henry said. "Violet has confessed everything."

"What?" Evelyn gasped.

"I woke up when Henry arrived and came downstairs when you both went into the kitchen," Violet said. "I listened behind the door." Her sudden little smile dared Evelyn to criticize her behavior as unladylike.

Evelyn swallowed her protest and listened instead.

"When I heard it wasn't Alex I had killed after all, I nearly fainted with relief, and almost burst in to confess right there. But then I kept listening, and what you and Henry had to say to each other made me think."

She released Alex's arm and stepped forward to take Evelyn's hands. "Did you really promise Mama to look after me?"

"Of course," Evelyn said. "She begged me on her deathbed. She said—she said you needed my steadiness."

Violet laughed and sighed at the same time. "Oh, Evie. Mama made *me* promise I would always look after you. She said you needed my zest for life, that otherwise you would grow too somber and stultified. So after her death I threw myself into providing your life with color and energy."

Evelyn put a hand to her head. "Oh mercy."

She saw it all now. The more wildly dramatic Vi grew, the more pinched and narrow Evelyn became; and the more coldly practical Evelyn was, the more Vi threw herself into emotion to try and balance it out.

Their mutual promises to their mother had almost succeeded in destroying both of them.

Vi took a step back and smiled proudly up at the tall gentleman by her side. "I needed to think about things a bit more before taking action—like you're always telling me to do —so I pretended to be asleep when you and Henry checked on me. Then I went and found Alex, told him the entire thing, and he brought me here to make my proper confession."

"So it seems your only crime lies in telling falsehoods to Deep officials, and since that is not magical in nature, it is out of our jurisdiction. Naturally some of my colleagues are rather annoyed at you—I wouldn't recommend doing anything to bring yourself to their attention for the next several months," Henry said. "Regardless, you may return home any time you please."

Evelyn licked her lips. "And—Violet?"

"I've already accepted the nine-month block," Vi said. "More than the minimum for my reckless carelessness, less than the maximum due to having never done anything of the sort before. Alex paid my fine. After all, we are engaged to be married."

Her fiancé spoke for the first time. "We will be married at once and then Vi will accompany me back to India. No one here in England need know of her block at all."

India! Evelyn mentally staggered. This was Vi taking responsibility for her life with a vengeance.

She would not repine or allow the plaintive query "but what about me?" to pass her lips. She would do nothing to spoil her sister's happiness and newfound maturity.

"Thank you," she said to them both instead. "I'm so happy for you."

Vi released Alex and came forward again to kiss her sister's cheek. "You could come with us to India, if you like," she said.

Evelyn hugged her briefly. "Thank you for your generosity, but I think it would be best for all of us if you and Alex were able to start your new life together on your own."

Over Vi's head, she saw the relief in Alex's face at her refusal. Vi dimpled and nodded in understanding. She, at least, seemed to find the mishap of the last ten years and its dramatic conclusion amusing.

At Henry, Evelyn did not dare to look.

"We're on our way to dinner with the Spencer family so we can announce our engagement to them," Vi said, beaming now. "Will you join us for that?"

"You know, I'm a little tired from all the excitement, Vi. I think I'll pass. You can tell me all about it tomorrow, will that do?"

Violet agreed that it would, and she and Alex left.

Evelyn mustered her courage and met Henry's gaze. She had told no untruth to her sister. She was utterly exhausted, drained from all the events of the day and the revelations. She wanted nothing more than to rush home and hide from the world, but she would not allow herself to show weakness before this man.

"I apologize for wasting your time with all of this. I don't suppose I may now know who it was Vi killed?"

Henry's face, as usual, showed nothing of his thoughts. "Part of that magical burglar gang you've all heard so many rumors about. He was their point man. He would disguise himself with a glamour to look like a respectable visitor and enter unoccupied houses openly during the day through the front door. There, he would lay down time-dictated spells to unlock the windows and doors later that night, as well as spells to find anything made of gold, silver, or precious stones within the house.

"We had barely caught onto his pattern but hadn't been able to catch him the act yet. It was his bad luck that he made the mistake of thinking you and Vi were out when he entered your house, and that he dropped the glamour in time for Vi to see him and defend herself. And it was her good luck that her reflexes were so quick, else he might have done her a real injury. These chaps hadn't so much as a scrap of conscience between them."

"Deep might have given her a short block, then," Evelyn said.

Henry shrugged. "They probably would have save for their irritation over how the two of you between you mucked up the case. As they couldn't take it out on you, they piled the penalty more strictly on her."

Evelyn felt even worse over her overblown act of supposed heroism at hearing that.

"I see," she said. "Thank you. Goodnight."

He hooked his thumbs in his waistcoat pockets and leaned back on his heels. "Martyring yourself again, my dear

Evelyn?"

She raised her chin. "Nothing of the sort. You've been proven right—as usual. Whether you'll believe me or not, I had decided to step back from interfering in Vi's life even before she and Alex came to tell me their tale. Only it turns out she's stepping out of mine instead, and that's even better for her. So I thank you for your insight, and I shall now remove myself from your life as well. Goodnight."

He caught up to her before she reached the door. "What if I don't want you out of my life?"

She didn't have the energy to argue. "Perhaps I want to be out of yours."

He raised one eyebrow. "Perhaps. If that is so, there's nothing more to be said. But I suspect you are sacrificing yourself again. You have decided your mistaken acting-out of your promise and the habits you've developed thereof have made you unfit for human companionship and so you will not allow yourself to get close to anyone again for fear you will start trying to control him or her."

"You must be right," Evelyn said, taking refuge in sarcasm. "You always are, after all."

Henry was already standing closer than propriety allowed, but he took another step forward, bringing him nearer yet. "My darling Evie, if you think for one moment either one of us will ever be able to squelch the other underfoot, you have a poor understanding of our personalities. I am the only person you could marry safely, because I will never let you nobly suffer for me. And you are the only woman in the world who could stand up to me when I start high-handedly running roughshod over you. Don't you see? We are more than the perfect match, we are each other's only *possible* match. For the sake of society, if nothing else, we must marry!"

The tension inside Evelyn that had been building all day released with a snap, bringing with it a gush of joy and burst of laughter rather than tears. She let go of the weight she'd been carrying for so long, far longer than this day.

Perhaps she did need some healthy selfishness in her life. Perhaps her mother had been right in her intent for the sisters to balance each other, however wrongly that had ended.

She would let go of her cold logic and for once let her emotions, though not control, her action.

"Very well," she said, shamelessly putting her arms around Henry's neck. "For the sake of saving society from the worst parts of each other's personalities, I will marry you."

To forestall whatever smug or self-satisfied pronouncement he was about to make, she kissed him with enough enthusiasm to make Violet blush, had she been there to see.

Masks & the

Magician

The Moscow night was bitterly cold and dark. The English magician calling himself Merlin crouched shivering outside the pillared and crenellated building. It had been at least three hours since he had taken his place here. His fur-lined gloves, boots, and hat had long since ceased to protect him from the bone-sinking chill.

Much as he tried to keep his mind on the job, he could not help but dwell longingly on thoughts of hot tea and toasted crumpets by the fire, preferably shared with a tall brunette with a hint of red in her hair, and eyes the color of sunlight on water, who laughed at him and challenged him all at the same time.

The magician sighed, a puff of fog in the bitter gloom. It had been months since he had arrived in Soviet Russia, long enough that all thoughts of his former life had faded nearly to a dream.

When he had first heard of the possible survival, through dark magic and darker deeds, of one of the Tsar's daughters, he had dismissed it as pure fantasy. Such rumors had swirled through the magical community ever since the Romanovs were murdered five years ago.

This one had started in the provinces and instead of fading away like all the rest, gained strength. Soon the whispers spread throughout Russia. This supposed Grand Duchess Anastasia convinced all she met of the validity of her claim.

The magician had to know the truth. He left England and spent weeks working his way into the Grand Duchess's inner circle. She and those closest to her were not inclined to trust an Englishman at first, but he had persuaded them of his merit. Everyone knew the English were romantics under their stoic exteriors; the Grand Duchess could easily believe that a man calling himself after the legendary kingmaker and sage Merlinus Ambrosius could be disillusioned with the sordid reality of post-war England and seeking to live out childhood dreams of glory and honor.

The money he donated to the cause helped as well.

It seemed something out of a fairy tale:

A grand duchess, caught in a dark spell, a curse thrown upon her by a loyal but misguided servant, a spell to obscure her true identity and allow her to escape her family's fate.

That same spell, now weaving itself into her soul, twisting and turning her while she strove with all the might of the Romanovs to resist it.

A handful of loyal followers, dedicated to bringing her to power and taking Russia back from its oppressors.

A lone Englishman to serve as her right hand, sworn to break the spell cast over her.

This vigil was no fairy tale, however. The magician was on his third night of waiting outside the home of a prominent member of the Bolshevik party, and he was beginning to think his efforts were futile.

After another hour of waiting for the lights to dim, and seeing them remain uncompromisingly bright, he deemed it time to give up for the night. He stamped his feet to get the blood moving in them, and trotted over to the other side of the entrance.

"I don't think we're going to make it tonight, either," he told the burly man hunched by the iron gate. "We need another plan."

Ivan only grunted.

He trailed after Merlin as they wound through the streets of Moscow. The Englishman shivered, wishing for an English pub and English beer and, heavens above, *tea*.

The Russians drank tea, but it wasn't the same. It was the company he missed the most.

Not but what he wasn't aware of the privilege of being here. This was something unprecedented, something that could shake the world. A Romanov daughter, alive? Russian power, changing hands? Even if ordinarily a female would never have inherited, the Grand Duchess seemed certain the people would rise up and cast out the Reds *and* the Whites once her curse was lifted and her identity made known.

Something like this would have repercussions all the way to England and beyond.

Still, it was cold and lonely, and so when he saw the man —even in the darkness the way he wore his overcoat marked him as a fellow Englishman—on the other side of the street vainly attempting to light a cigarette, Merlin didn't think twice about crossing over and offering him a light.

He didn't smoke himself, of course—people who were born with a sensitivity to magic also had a sensitivity to cigarette and cigars, something magician-scientists still couldn't entirely explain—but he carried a lighter all the same. It helped one blend in better with the general population.

"Thanks," said the other Englishman, watching the smoke rise from the lighted cigarette tip. "Cold night."

"Too cold," Merlin answered back.

A grunt behind him reminded him of Ivan, there not only as an aid but also a guard. Some of the Grand Duchess's advisors were still suspicious of an Englishman. Merlin was not allowed out anywhere without someone to keep an eye of him.

"Well, good night," he said lightly, and continued along his way.

As he turned the corner of the street, he saw the other Englishman toss his cigarette down to the street and grind it out under his heel, without ever having raised it to his lips.

Merlin half smiled and kept walking.

He and Ivan followed a devious route of alleyways and side streets before finally reaching the abandoned warehouse the Grand Duchess had adopted for her center of operations in Moscow.

Here, as in the village where Merlin had met her, she sat in a chair in the center of the room, in this case the large, echoing warehouse chamber, and dominated all the activity by her stillness.

Tall, dark of hair and eye, with strong features and a bosom an opera singer would have killed to possess, she had a presence that hit one between the eyes, leaving one dazed and all-too willing to serve her smallest whim. It was no wonder so many had already flocked to her banner, and she was convinced even more would once her true identity was established.

"Another failed attempt?" she said as the two men entered the room, her rich, musical voice cutting through the low buzz of conversation echoing among the rafter.

That buzz died away as all eyes turned toward the men.

"The colonel keeps late hours, your Imperial Highness," Merlin said with an apologetic bow. "By the time the lights have gone off inside, the street outside is busy with dawn activity." He coughed and continued. "Not to say I wouldn't be willin' to try, don't you know, but it'd be a terrible shame if

I got caught with the, er, goods and they never made it to you in the end. Poor show, all for lack of foresight on my part, what?"

"Indeed," said the Grand Duchess. Merlin relaxed a trifle. "We must think of another approach."

This was his cue.

"Well," he said, scratching his head. "I did have a bit of a thought."

"Shocking," one of the advisors muttered.

Merlin huffed and turned a deaf ear to the man.

"I don't know if it would work, but I just thought of it. Out of the blue, y'know, while I was watchin' the house. Or rather, out of the black, on account of it bein' night and all."

"And what was that idea?" asked the Grand Duchess, impatience heavy in her tone.

Merlin fought the urge to apologize for wasting her time and reveal all his hopes and plans, even those not concerning her. Her effect on him was growing the more time he spent in her presence.

"Well, with all these meetings the colonel is constantly havin' with other high-up Bolshevik officials, breakin' in from the outside seems out of the question. But if I could get m'self invited inside, it would be almost too easy."

"How would you get such an invitation?"

Merlin blinked a few times. "A wealthy Englishman in Moscow meets up with the colonel, starts chattin' about what a splendid job the Reds are doin' in Russia, lays it on nice and thick, mentions how this lovely Russian lady has been tellin' him all about the cultural gatherings they have here, with poetry and music and serious discussions and all that, and how superior that seems to the English frivolity he's escaped back home, but that he hasn't been able to attend any such ... seems the colonel would almost have to arrange such a gathering, so the Englishman and his Russian lady friend could attend and the Englishman gain a good impression to take back home with him."

"It seems plausible," said the Grand Duchess, over the immediate objections of her advisors. "I believe it could work. Who would be the lady?"

Merlin grinned at her, made reckless by success. "Fancy a bit of an outing, your Imperial Highness?"

***

As he'd expected, the advisors hated the idea. Merlin thought he'd have to be more persuasive, but the Grand Duchess, surprisingly, agreed at once.

"It is my right," she said, ruthlessly overriding the advisors' objections. "The jewels are mine, stolen from the body of the maid who took on my appearance and was killed in my place. The power of the Romanovs is in them. The instant I touch them, I will gain the strength of my ancestors and be able to break the shackles of this curse once and for all. Where better to resume my proper self and start my path to the throne than in the house of my enemy who stole the jewels in the first place?"

It was not her logic that convinced them in the end, but rather the sheer weight of her personality. Their arguments grew feebler and feebler, and ended altogether when she surged out of her chair, fists clenched at her sides and her head thrown back proudly.

"Enough! Am I not your ruler? Will I not be Tsarina soon? Who are you to tell me what I must and must not do? I say I will go to this party and I will break my own curse rather than relying on others to do it for me. Merlin, you will go today to introduce yourself to the colonel. Annushka, you will procure me a proper gown. Ivan, you will accompany Merlin."

Merlin blinked lazily at her. "I've no objection to Ivan's company, your Imperial Highness, but won't it look rather suspicious if I'm followed everywhere by a giant Russian?"

"He will stay hidden," she said, waving a dismissive hand. "He has magic enough for that."

Merlin shrugged. "As you wish."

Despite everything, the Grand Duchess didn't really trust him. Ivan was there to make sure he said or did nothing out of place, nothing that might betray their plans.

That was all right. He wasn't planning anything untoward. He would give the Grand Duchess exactly what she asked for.

After a brief nap, Merlin left the warehouse again, trailed as usual by Ivan, who made good use of a chameleon spell to blend into the background as Merlin directed his steps toward the colonel's residence. He had timed it just right, crossing paths with him exactly as the colonel closed his front door and stepped into the street. Merlin flung out his hands and gasped expressively, showing surprise and dismay as he bumped into the portly man and spilled his papers all over the street.

"Oh goodness me, terribly sorry, can't think how I got so clumsy, mea culpa and all that," Merlin said, scrambling to pick up documents and scraps of paper before they blew away. He handed the pile back to the colonel with a little bow. "Must be this Moscow weather," he said.

"Yes," the colonel answered stiffly. "It is always cold in

January."

Merlin altered his path to walk beside the colonel, chattering amiably about this and that. By the time they reached the army headquarters, the little Russian had relaxed enough to fall in with Merlin's scheme. He issued the invitation to a "cultural experience" the very next night for "the Honorable Frederick Winters and his guest," and Merlin, hoping the real Freddie Winters would never hear of this borrowing of his name, expressed his extreme gratitude.

That taken care of, the colonel went about his business and Merlin did the same, rejoining the only-vaguely-there Ivan with a satisfied smile.

"I think that went well, don't you?"

The big Russian only grunted.

Merlin shook his head sadly. "You have no appreciation for a truly artistic lie, my friend."

As they left the vicinity, Merlin paused to rescue a young woman's handbag from the gutter where she had dropped it as he approached.

"Allow me, madam," he said gallantly, returning it to her with a bow.

She made no answer, merely nodding her thanks and walking off with a stride more closely resembling a man's than a woman's.

Merlin turned his thoughts away from the willowy glide of English ladies and focused it back on business.

This had been the easy part. The next evening would be the real test.

***

By the next evening, everything was in place. The Grand

Duchess wore a magnificent pre-Revolution style gown of black velvet which had surely originally come from Paris. Merlin's own formal wear was impeccable, but next to her his broad shoulders, sleeked-back hair, and indefinable air of English gentry faded in comparison.

He did the best he could on his white tie, but he sorely felt the lack of his valet.

Leaving behind the still-protesting advisors and followers, the two swept arm-in-arm out of the warehouse and onto the streets, paying no attention to the multitude of curious looks they garnered as they walked the distance to the colonel's residence. Merlin thought at one point he saw the same young lady whose bag he had picked up earlier, but she darted back into the crowd when he turned his head, and he dismissed it from his mind.

They entered the colonel's brick house along with a crowd of other guests, two more faces in the midst of many.

The Grand Duchess couldn't remain an anonymous part of any crowd for long. Side glances turned into outright stares, and whispers arose on either side as she swept through the entryway and into the main part of the house, where musicians sat tuning their instruments and poets stood in corners eating the colonel's food and glaring at each other.

Judging by her half-closed eyes and faint smile, she was well aware of and well satisfied with her effect. Merlin, English to the core, felt something of a fool.

The colonel bustled up to them.

"Welcome, Comrade Winters, and welcome to your friend! I don't believe we have met, Comrade ...?"

The Grand Duchess favored him with one of her imperious stares. "No, we have not met, Colonel."

She turned her back on him in a piece of deliberate rudeness and walked away.

Merlin needed no acting ability to bring up the crimson color in his cheeks. "Er ... terribly, ah, terribly sorry, sir, er, Comrade. Can't imagine what came over her."

The colonel frowned. "It seems I am the one who must apologize. I have offended her?"

"I couldn't say, I'm sure," was all Merlin could offer. "Er, excuse me."

He cut through the crowd and caught up with the Grand Duchess at the edge of the room. "What were you thinking, insulting our host like that?" he demanded in as fierce a tone as he could manage while still keeping his voice low.

She turned her eyes on him and his knees nearly buckled under the weight of her displeasure. "The man is a thief and a murderer as well as a traitor to the throne. He has in his possession jewels that belong to *me*, to my family. If he was not one of the soldiers involved in their deaths, he has benefited from it. I have no reason to treat him with anything but contempt. If I could, I would spit upon him."

"You could remember our purpose here," Merlin said. "How can we, er, liberate the jewels if everyone is staring at you and talking about you? Half the room heard your jab at him!"

Had it been possible for her to produce such a low expression, Merlin would have said she smirked. "My dear Merlin—or should I call you Mr. Winters? The Honorable Frederick Winters?—it is all part of the plan, is it not? While everyone is noticing me, no one will see you leave this room for the colonel's study. When you bring me the jewels and they allow me to break this curse, the revelation of my identity will be all the greater for this scene now."

Her use of the name he had given to the colonel was deliberate. He had not shared that name with anyone in the Grand Duchess's court. She knew who he was, she was saying, and she would not hesitate to use that against him.

In return, he dropped his amiably idiotic mask. "I'm surprised you trust me. Aren't you worried I'll scarper with the jewels if you aren't there when I remove them from the safe? I don't see Ivan anywhere here to stop me."

Her frown was fierce and sudden. "You wouldn't dare!"

"Maybe I would, maybe I wouldn't. You can't really know, can you?"

"I will hunt you down and tear out your throat with my bare hands if you betray me!"

Merlin resisted the urge to step back. He had faced worse opponents than she. The urge to yield to her pressure was not natural. Prickles ran up and down his spine, and he chose his next words carefully.

"Why would I betray you? I just can't help feeling you're thinking of betraying me."

The flicker in her eyes gave her away. "What an absurd notion."

"I'm sure it is. Yet this is starting to feel like a set-up. With me, as they say in the States, as the fall guy."

A muscle in her cheek jumped. "You insult me with such a suggestion."

He wanted to suggest she commiserate with the colonel over being insulted, but he held his tongue. The next move was hers.

As they had been speaking in heated but quiet English, most of the room's occupants couldn't understand them.

That they were arguing would be obvious to all, but Merlin hoped it would appear they were still discussing her rudeness to the colonel. If anyone else got a hint of what they were up to, they would both be summarily imprisoned. He, for one, had no desire to discover what Russian prisons were like.

As he remained silent, the Grand Duchess pressed the back of her hand to her forehead. "Ah!" she exclaimed. "It is too hot—all these people! I am faint. I must rest."

Merlin suppressed the urge to roll his eyes. He slid back into his role of devoted suitor. "Oh dear," he said, flinging his arm around her waist for support. "I'll get you a chair."

She half-swooned against him, the beads on her dress's bodice pressing into his arm and chest. "No—no—I must lie down. A sofa, Comrade Winters. Not a chair."

Taking his cue, he hustled her past the guests now openly staring at the spectacle the two of them made, through the doorway leading to the rest of the house, and into the second room on the left: the colonel's study.

As soon as they entered the room, the Grand Duchess pulled away.

"There," she said. "Now neither of us can double-cross the other."

He smiled at her. "You are a magnificent actress, Your Imperial Highness."

She glanced sharply at him, as though searching for a hidden meaning behind his words, but he turned away to lock the door with a simple spell, showing an unresponsive back in answer to her look.

The room was simply furnished and decorated: thick red curtains covering the windows, wood crackling in the fireplace, sturdy chairs clustered around a large oak desk with papers littering the top. The Grand Duchess's eyes lingered on that as she seated herself in one of the chairs.

"Go on then, *Merlin*," she said, pointing to the lone piece of artwork on the wall: a painting of St. Petersburg at night in winter, looking incongruous in this sparse room. "Prove to me your loyalty."

He swept her a low bow. "This evening shall show to you my true nature, I trust."

He unhooked the painting and set it on the floor, revealing the flat grey metal door it had so blatantly covered.

Merlin was no safecracker, but he knew a few spells to unlock doors. Affecting an air of unconcern, he leaned against the wall beside the safe, one hand resting at the small of his back with fingers splayed and thumb tucked into his palm, and sent out an exploratory spell to see what sort of a lock he was dealing with.

He straightened, grinning, when the spell brought back its results. This was going to be even easier than he'd thought. Rather than a spell to remove the door or the lock, both of which took a certain amount of energy to maintain, he instead murmured, "*Aggravare*."

Infinitesimal particles in the air floated down to gather in a ball above his open palm. It was not visible to the naked eye, but it glowed bronze in Len's other sense—the sense which was called *magic* by those who had it and had learned to use it.

When he judged it heavy enough, he directed the bronze ball to the top of the safe door and drove it home.

The weight of the *gravis* ball was not enough to smash the door, but that was not its purpose. It jarred the lock just enough to knock loose the locking pin, causing the door to fall open on its own. They could close the door after they were finished and the colonel would never know the safe had been opened—until he found his jewels missing.

Merlin stepped back and bowed. "Your jewels, Your Imperial Highness."

The Grand Duchess's eyes glittered like gems themselves and she rose from her chair. "This," she declaimed, "is a wonderful moment. It is the dawning of a new age for Russia. Bring me my jewels, Merlin!"

The Englishman stretched his hand into the safe, then withdrew it still empty. "Wouldn't you rather be the first to touch them, Your Imperial Highness? Seems more symbolic and all that, y'know. 'No more shall foreign fingers soil the jewels of my people' and so on and so forth."

He hoped she wouldn't ask the source of the quotation, since he had made it up on the spot.

"Yes," she decided, throwing her head back. "You are correct. Out of my way!"

She swept forward and he obligingly fell back toward the window to make room, resting on hand on the edge of the crimson curtain.

The Grand Duchess reached into the safe. A look of triumph painted itself on her face as she pulled out a lumpy bag, bringing it to her chest.

"And now—" she began.

"And now," Merlin interrupted. "You are under arrest."

He swept the curtain back to reveal three men: two Russian magicians and one nondescript Englishman. Ivan might have seen in the Englishman a trace of the man whose cigarette Merlin had lighted the other evening, and the young woman whose handbag Merlin had rescued the day before, but Ivan was not there.

Before the Grand Duchess could do more than draw breath, a gauzy light emanated from the bag, weaving itself around her body to obscure her face and form.

"What have you done?" she screamed at Merlin.

"Only what you wanted," he said. "The magic in the items in that bag are undoing the black magic that has you in its grip."

She writhed and twisted, but could not escape the glowing cocoon until the light faded on its own, leaving the woman within revealed for her true self at last.

She looked no different at first glance. Still statuesque, still with dark hair and eyes and strong features, still lovely save for the rage stamped across her face.

But gone was the indefinable air of command, the allurement that drew all eyes to her, the aura that could make any man, even one as unsusceptible as Merlin want to fall at her feet in worship. She stood apart from her magic, an ordinary woman at last.

Not a Romanov.

"How dare you?" she screeched, lunging for her erstwhile Merlin.

The two Russians intercepted her before her carmine-tipped fingers could tear at his throat.

"No you don't, Marya Alexandrovna," said the one. "We've been watching you for a long time, and now, thanks to this man, we have you."

The lady stopped struggling. "You knew the entire time?"

The Englishman met her furious glare coldly. "That you were a thief after the colonel's jewels? Oh yes. My manservant and I have been communicating ever since I joined your merry band of cutthroats and robbers."

"Impossible! Ivan—"

Merlin smiled, letting his contempt show through at long last. Lord, but he was tired of wearing this mask. "Ivan never even noticed. The colonel was in on it, too. These gentlemen," nodding at the Russian magicians, "warned him there was going to be a robbery attempt. I gave the code words when I introduced myself to him—also under Ivan's nose—and he agreed to leave his study unguarded tonight so we could catch you in the act. Your little scene out front was most helpful. I wasn't sure how to keep you out there while these three swapped out the real jewels with the spell-breaking bag, re-locked the safe, and hid themselves. We had to rid you of that allurement spell you were using before anyone could be trusted to bring you to justice."

The second Russian magician addressed him. "It was a strong spell, Comrade. How did you resist it?"

For the last five years, a magical and mysterious con artist and thief in Russia had defeated every magician sent after her. When rumors started to swirl of a resurrected Grand Duchess, the magical authorities suspected it was the same woman, but they were reluctant to lose any more magicians to her.

Enter "Merlin," conveniently transferred to the British Magicians' Embassy at the right moment, a magician with a particular knack for shielding against curses and other dark magic and a useful manservant accompanying him.

Perhaps feeling they would rather lose an English magician than one of their own, the Russians let him have his head.

He shrugged. "Just lucky, I guess." His eyes dwelled a moment longer on the struggling, swearing woman before turning his head in one final gesture of disgust. "You'll want to check her over. I'm fairly certain she stole some papers off the desk while I cracked the safe. Probably hoping to blackmail the colonel with them."

"You swine," she said with venom.

"Madam, it takes one to know one," he replied.

***

Back at the British Magicians' Embassy (a tiny room tucked away within the Moscow British Embassy, ignored and unnoticed by the general staff), the two Englishmen relaxed in front of a fireplace, with hot tea and crumpets at hand.

The man no longer known as Merlin *or* the Honorable Frederick Winters shook his head. "Tea and crumpets! Becket, you're a wonder. However did you manage to procure these in Soviet Moscow?"

Becket smiled as he presented his employer with a perfectly toasted and buttered crumpet. "I have my sources, sir."

Lennox Davies, magician, English gentleman, and undercover agent with British Magical Intelligence, gladly accepted the crumpet from his manservant's hand. "I should know better by now than to question you." His contented sigh came all the way from his booted toes. "At last this blasted job is done and we can go home! Home to England, eh, and no longer having to live in the shadows."

"At least until your next assignment," Becket corrected.

Len's sigh this time was not so content. This job, important as it was, grew more onerous each year. "At least we got her," he said.

Alarmed by the possibility of a world leader corrupted by

dark magic, Len's superiors had sent him to Russia under the guise of an attaché to the magical ambassador with orders to discover the truth and stop this woman, whoever she may be, from taking the throne. They would be pleased with his report, though not, perhaps, with how long the job had taken.

"If I may ask, sir, were you never deceived by her or affected by the allurement spell, even for a moment? Forgive me if I overstep my bounds, but it is impressive, even with your training."

Len took a sip of tea, his mind going back to the summer of 1909, when he had been forced to accompany his mother to the Queen's garden party during a visit to England by the Romanovs. He was sixteen, bored and irritated to be in his good clothes with a lot of stuffy folk instead of out playing rugby. When he'd been accosted by the eight-year-old Grand Duchess Anastasia, equally bored and looking for mischief, he'd been more amused than anything. By the time he'd answered her unending questions—how Len's family treated their tenants on their family estate in Wales, what British servants were like, what was his favorite sport, and so on—and narrowly beaten her in the footrace she'd challenged him to, he had forgotten his boredom and amusement alike, and the two were fast friends.

The core of a person didn't change, in Len's opinion. Despite war, captivity, and suffering, the bright-eyed girl in a white lace dress who had been genuinely interested in the proper way to treat one's dependents, who was loyal to a fault, fearless to the point of recklessness, filled with passion for life ... one could change a person's appearance through magic, change their outer nature through misery and hardship, but he knew of nothing that could change who a person really was.

He'd known from the first few moments of meeting the imposter that she could not possibly be the real Anastasia, and her deception had filled him with such fury that he had determined to bring her down in the most humiliating way possible, to strip away her mask in the moment of her greatest triumph.

It wasn't particularly sportsmanlike. It wasn't professional —his superiors would have been appalled by him allowing the personal to creep in like that.

At end of that garden party thirteen years ago, the true Grand Duchess Anastasia had thanked him for a most enjoyable afternoon.

"I am glad to think I have made an English friend," she had said, her laughing eyes a contrast to her grave face and careful words.

"The next time we meet I'll teach you to play rugby," he had promised.

She had laughed, and that was his last memory of her— laughter and sunshine in one narrow, pointed face.

He couldn't regret the way he had brought about the fall of Marya Alexandrovna.

"No," he finally answered Becket's question. "She never took me in. Not even for a moment."

He was weary to his bones, worn out by more than simply the cold and the hardships of the job, but the memory of Anastasia Romanova reminded him of why he did this job. He had not been able to save her from her murderers, but at least he had kept her name from being tarnished.

He didn't work to keep England alone safe, but to protect and defend the innocent people who had no voice of their

own. That was both his privilege and his responsibility.
     He could do no less.

The End

A note from the author:

Thank you for reading these short stories! I hope you enjoyed them. Thanks go out to A.M. Offenwanger, critique partner extraordinaire, Laura Rizzo and Heather Elliot for beta reading and editing suggestions, and to all the readers who have kept faith even as year after year did not produce the sequel to 2013's *Magic Most Deadly*. These stories are for you!

And now, to give you a taste of that sequel so many of you have waited so patiently for, here is the first chapter of Book 2 of the Whitney & Davies series, titled *Glamour & Gunshots*, due to come out sometime in 2018.

Happy Reading!

Glamours & Gunshots

Whitney and Davies

Book 2

by E.L. Bates

This excerpt is from a work in progress and may not reflect perfectly the finished product

DEAD MAN WALKING

✳

Merry birdsong filled the air on that bright April morning when the dead man stumbled into Aunt Amelia's front hall.

Technically, he was dying, not dead, else he couldn't have stumbled anywhere; corpses, in general, being no longer animate. There was just enough time for Maia, passing through the hall on her way to the rose parlor for a magic lesson with Aunt Amelia, to drop her books and papers and dash forward, catching the man in her arms beneath the butler's outraged nose.

"Call a doctor!" she cried, but it was too late. The man's eyelids fluttered and he breathed a single word:

"*Beware.*"

Then he sighed and expired.

It was so ridiculously like something out of a dime novel that Maia couldn't believe it was real. She looked up, half expecting a beautiful foreign adventuress in furs and jewels to next appear in the hall, followed by a leering, greasy-haired scoundrel waving a gun.

All she saw, however, was the sagging jaw and round eyes in the face of Mr. Lorde, her aunt's ever-so-dignified butler. That, and the limp weight in her arms, convinced her this was no hoax. She'd seen dead bodies before—held men as they died, in her time in France—and recognized the reality of the situation, however absurd it seemed.

"Mr. Lorde," she said in a soft voice most unusual for her. "I believe you should fetch my aunt. At once." She set the man down on the polished floor, careful not to disturb him more than necessary. Her decorous side wished to close his staring eyes; her practical side warned her the scene should be as little disturbed as possible.

"Yes, miss," the butler said, closing his mouth and swallowing hard. "And the doctor, miss?"

"No need for one anymore," she said, not taking her eyes from the dead man's face. "The police are more likely—or Domestic Protection—but Aunt Amelia first."

The butler positively scurried out of the room, a sight to delight anyone who bothered to notice, and Maia set to work. The light was poor in the entryway, thanks to the ridiculous stained glass windows above the door preventing sunlight from properly entering, so she murmured a spell to assist her task. Aunt Amelia did not approve of apprentices using magic unsupervised, but Maia had mastered this particular spell before she even began her apprenticeship, and this was an emergency.

"*Lux fiat*," she said, and a ball of steady silver light sprang to life above her open palm. Maia directed it to hover over the body while she began her examination. Aunt Amelia wouldn't approve of this, either, but some tasks Maia preferred not to entrust to others.

With steady hands, she patted him down, checking his pockets and examining his body. It didn't take long; he was a short, sturdy man, dressed in middle-class clothing consisting of unkempt trousers and a collared shirt, though missing a coat and tie. No identification on him, no incriminating papers, nothing helpful at all. After she finished, she sat back on her heels, frowning. "*Finiatur*," she said absently, and the silver light vanished.

In her experience, people who died from an illness were

not usually waltzing around London immediately before so doing, and there were usually tell-tale signs of said illness left behind. On the other hand, people who died from violence generally bore the traces of their wound. This man was unmarked and appeared in perfect health, aside from the fact that he was dead.

Maia did not believe in jumping to conclusions. Still, she thought it a reasonable assumption that magic was most likely behind this. After all, he had come to Aunt Amelia's house to die. Amelia Rawlings was well-known throughout Europe—the magical population thereof, at least—as one of the finest magicians of her generation.

The front door swung, causing Maia to jump and search her mind for a defensive spell. She relaxed when the newcomer proved to be a dark-skinned, dark-haired young lady dressed in the very latest spring fashions, her curly hair covered with a modish cloche and her black eyes sparkling.

"Hope you don't mind," she called as she sashayed through the doorway. "It was open ..." The words died in her throat as she took in the incongruous tableau.

It must have been an absurd sight. The brown-and-gold papered walls of the entryway, Maia in her unfashionable but practical working costume of brown checked skirt and cream short-sleeved blouse, the second housemaid frozen in the background with her mouth open in a silent scream, and the dead body on the spotless floor.

"Good morning, Helen," Maia said.

Aunt Amelia, trailed by a still-shaken Lorde, popped out of the rose parlor at that exact moment. Old woman and young both opened their mouths and said,

"Maia Whitney, what have you done now?"

It was the "now" that really irritated Maia. It wasn't as if she made a habit of collecting dead bodies and stirring up general mayhem. True, there had been that one occasion, but that was nearly four years ago, and none of it had been her fault. Well, maybe one or two bits of it, but ...

"This is none of my doing," she said, rising to her feet and striving to keep her voice from sounding petulant. She wasn't certain she entirely succeeded. "He came in and dropped dead at my feet. Aunt, it's your house. Do you recognize him?"

Aunt Amelia came closer and peered down at him. "No," she said. "Mr. Lorde?"

The butler didn't move. "Madam?" he said. Maia detected a note of pleading under that stiff word.

"Oh, don't be such a coward, Lorde," Aunt Amelia said. "Come here and look at the fellow and tell me if you know him. He's dead, he's not going to jump up and bite your nose off."

When Lorde had reluctantly obeyed and disclaimed any knowledge of him, to be thankfully dismissed, Helen approached to take her turn as well.

"You're not likely to know him," Aunt Amelia objected.

"You never know," Helen said. "I made no secret of my intentions to come here and spend the morning with Maia. Maybe it was me he was trying to reach!" She stood next to Maia and looked down. "Is he really dead? He looks so peaceful." She sighed. "No, I don't recognize him, either. What do we do now?"

"I think he might have died of a magic spell," Maia said. "There's no sign of injury or illness on him."

Aunt Amelia pursed her lips. "Checked that already, did you?"

"I did," Maia returned. Her aunt did not speak, but Maia thought she saw some approval beneath the surface frown. Though it might have been wishful thinking. Her aunt seemed to approve of independent thought and deed in everyone but her niece-apprentice.

Helen backed away from the body a few steps and made a faint noise in the back of her throat. The sparkle in her eyes dimmed. "Sorry," she said weakly when the other two looked at her. "Don't mind me. I just ... it suddenly struck me that this is real."

"I know," Maia said, smiling at her friend with sympathy. Helen was twenty-one, four years younger than Maia, and Maia had lied about her age to get into the VADs when she was seventeen. This was likely the first time her energetic, effervescent friend had ever seen a dead body outside the cinema. "It seemed unbelievable to me at first, too."

Aunt Amelia turned her frown on Helen. "Why are you here, anyway, Miss Radcliffe?"

"The Magicians' Ball is at the end of the week, remember, Miss Rawlings? Maia and I were going to go shopping for new gowns today."

That wasn't exactly the case: when the two girls had met for tea last week, Helen had said, "Oh Maia, we must get new frocks for the Magicians' Ball," and Maia had said, "I don't think so, Helen," and Helen had said, "Good, I'll pick you up Friday morning and we can visit Mme Julie's." Maia had protested that she had lessons with Aunt Amelia every morning, and Helen had waved that objection aside as breezily as she did everything else.

It wasn't that Maia despised the thought of a new gown, by any means. It was rather that she had entered her fourth

year of magical apprenticeship to her aunt and was
determined to not let it go into a fifth. She had discovered her
magical ability much later in life than most, and while she was
deeply thankful to have use of this extra sense at all, she was
beginning to chafe under her aunt's rules and restrictions,
especially while people younger and—she had to say it, even if
it sounded vain—less talented than she were already
journeymen or independent magicians. Somehow, gown
shopping for her fourth Magician's Ball as an apprentice did
not appeal. Helen, however, was determined to keep Maia
from "depression of spirits," as she airily put it, and therefore
insisted on regular outings and excursions. Maia appreciated
her efforts and at the same time found them maddening.

Aunt Amelia, who did despise new gowns (Maia did not
think she had purchased one since Queen Victoria sat on the
throne), waved her hand. "Yes, yes," she said. "Excellent idea.
Lessons canceled for today, Maia. You girls run along and
have fun."

Maia stared. Aunt Amelia seemed unaware of her niece's
scrutiny as she bent closer to the dead man, but the set of her
shoulders told Maia a different story. "Excuse me, Aunt."

Aunt Amelia looked up, a faint line appearing between
her eyebrows. "Maia, I am preparing to cast a highly delicate
spell, in order to find out what killed this unfortunate man,
do you mind not making me lose the threads?"

"Terribly sorry," said Maia, not feeling particularly sorry at
all. "But don't you think this is the sort of thing your
apprentice ought to assist with?"

"Or ... I'm sorry, but should we be doing anything about
this at all?" interrupted Helen. She actually did sound
apologetic. "Shouldn't we call Domestic Protection?"

"That useless excuse for a magical police force?" Aunt Amelia said, her bosom shaking with outrage. "In my house?"

Maia was reluctant to hand such a juicy mystery over to the authorities, but she had to admit Helen had a point. "She might be right, Aunt."

Do her justice, Aunt Amelia was stubborn and set in her ways, but she wasn't stupid. "Allow me to diagnose what killed him first. That will give us a better idea of who we need to bring in." She held up a finger. "And you girls may watch, but do not interfere. Especially you, Maia! I have no desire to add a house fire to the list of this day's calamities."

It took all Maia's self-control to keep from blushing. Just because her powers tended to ... explode out of her control at times was no call for Aunt Amelia to make a crack like that. It wasn't as if Maia was continually setting fire to the furniture, after all. She hadn't had an accident in at least three and a half months.

Besides, it was galling to have her master poke at her in front of another magician, even one with whom Maia was so friendly as Helen. Masters were supposed to brag about and defend their apprentices from others' ridicule, not expose them.

Thankfully, Helen ignored Aunt Amelia's comment except to move a step or two closer to Maia's side, as if to show she had no fear of Maia letting loose with an explosion. Aunt Amelia turned her back to both of them, raised her hands above her head, and spoke clearly and crisply in Latin.

"*Quid occursum est.*"

A wave of revulsion so strong it nearly drove her to her knees hit Maia like a fist. Beside her, Helen gagged and doubled over, hands clasped to her mouth. Aunt Amelia herself stumbled back, face ashen.

"*Finiatur!*" she boomed.

As though someone had flipped a switch, the revulsion vanished. Helen slowly straightened and pulled her hands back down to her sides.

"What ... what was that?" she managed to choke out.

Aunt Amelia examined her own hands, as though checking for contamination. Maia realized that she herself had not only touched that body, but had held it in her lap. Her skin crawled, and she had to resist the urge to scrub at her arms.

"That man died of one of the vilest forms of sorcery I've ever come across, and that's saying something," Aunt Amelia said. "That body needs to be burned at once."

"No, we mustn't," Maia said, then bit her lip. If it was bad form for a master to criticize her apprentice in front of others, it was even worse for an apprentice to contradict her master.

Aunt Amelia was never predictable. Instead of scolding Maia, she folded her arms across her ample bosom. "And why not? Why should I leave a body leaking the vilest of magics lying in my front hall?"

"We must know where it came from, what happened, who he is," Maia said. "What if it's not a spell, but rather a magical plague? Or if it is a spell, surely we must find out who cast it, and why, and bring him or her to justice. We cannot do that if we burn the body and lose all the clues it might contain."

"Looking for an excuse to play detective, child?" Aunt Amelia said, the sarcasm in her voice sharp enough to cut.

Maia clenched her fist, driving her nails into her palm until the desire to scream faded. She was twenty-five years old, hardly a child. And while Aunt Amelia scorned her fondness for detective novels and occasional ventures into solving puzzles in real life, Maia was proud of her deductive abilities. She and her friend Lennox Davies spent many a happy half-hour going over newspaper accounts of various crimes and trying to solve them. Len, an undercover agent for Magical Intelligence, had vastly more experience, but Maia's attention to detail and logical approach to criminology kept the honors about even between them.

Not that Aunt Amelia knew about those clandestine meetings. Len was perfectly respectable, but Aunt Amelia had a personal dislike toward him and also considered him a distraction to her niece's studies. Their occasional tea at Lyons had to be carried out with ridiculous secrecy. Maia refused to let her aunt dictate her personal relationships, though. Apprenticeship only went so far.

Before Maia lost her temper and self-control entirely, Aunt Amelia spoke again.

"Very well, I suppose we'd better call in the authorities." She heaved an enormous sigh. "I shall never live this down—common investigators, in my house!"

"Miss Rawlings, you know my brother Matthew has just started with Domestic Protection," Helen said. "If you like, I can summon him. He might be able to arrange things so that your privacy is protected."

Aunt Amelia eyed her with surprise and rare approval. "That is most thoughtful, Helen, thank you."

Helen nodded and withdrew into the rose parlor to cast the summoning spell which would let her brother know he was needed urgently at this location. Maia and her aunt were left alone.

"This is quite inconvenient," Aunt Amelia said, staring at

the body.

Maia raised her eyebrows. Death and black magic were hardly what she would call "inconvenient." Deadly, dangerous, and disastrous, yes. A minor irritant, no.

"There is trouble brewing between France and England," Aunt Amelia continued, answering the unspoken question. "A scandal involving an English magician and a French non-magical nobleman ... the Circle and the French Société are at each other's throats over this. The Circle has been threatening to send me over to discipline our magician lest the French take it into their heads to do it for us, though given the provocation I find my sympathies are entirely with him."

"That is all very interesting, no doubt, but hardly to be compared with a mysterious dead body leaking some sort of vile spell in your hallway, Aunt!"

"My dear child, it is matters such as this that can lead to wars. Should the French governing body of magicians attempt to imprison or punish an English magician, it would be a breach of agreement between all the magical governments of the world and could splinter us into factions, bringing up long-buried grievances individual alliances. It could be another worldwide war, only this time between magicians. Compared to that, a dead body in my hallway is indeed a sordid inconvenience."

Put like that, Maia could understand her aunt's point of view. On the other hand, as she looked at the crumpled figure and recalled the weight of it in her arms in that moment of change between a living human being and an empty corpse, she couldn't help but think that though his death might not spark a war, he too was important, and he deserved more than impatience and disgust.

***

Within a short time of Helen's summons to her brother—either he was extraordinarily protective of his sister or her summons had had an extra edge of urgency about it—England's magical police force had arrived at Aunt Amelia's residence in all its glory. "All its glory," in this case, consisted of a worried-looking Matthew Radcliffe and a grey-haired elderly woman with tired eyes who was introduced as Mrs. Taylor, their curse expert.

Matthew was tall and sturdily built, not resembling his sister much at all beyond the curly hair he tried and failed to tame under a hat, and a shared determination around both their mouths. Where her dark eyes sparkled, his were clouded and grim, and where she seemed to shed light wherever she walked, he seemed under a darkness. Maia suspected it was the nature of the work that did that to him, though he was old enough he might have had a few months to a year in the War, as well.

Matthew and Mrs. Taylor gaped in mutual dismay at the corpse. Whatever latent curse Aunt Amelia's diagnostic spell had triggered had only grown stronger in the time since it was set off; no one could now bear to go within a five-foot radius of the man.

"This is beyond my abilities," Mrs. Taylor admitted in a shaken voice.

"Fortunately for you, it is not beyond ours," said a sharp, ice-cold voice from the front door.

All heads turned as a short, thin man with a pinched face and a tall woman stepped into the hall. Behind them, a man so insignificant as to be almost unnoticeable carefully closed the door.

"Agent Barry, Agent Marsh," the man said, introducing themselves with a careless wave of the hand. "Magical Intelligence."

Aunt Amelia shot a glare at Maia, who spread her hands in innocence. If she had contacted Intelligence, which she hadn't, she would have gone straight to Len. Not this man.

"I don't recall inviting Intelligence to look into this affair," Aunt Amelia said, her bosom swelling with offended dignity.

"You didn't, yet here we are." Agent Barry glanced around the room, looked down at the corpse, over at Matthew and Mrs. Taylor, and sniffed, the edge of his upper lip curling. "This curse is far beyond the abilities or jurisdiction of Domestic Protection. Clearly this is no petty curse-caster. A spell of this nature could have implications for national security, or could even be part of an international plot."

"Though we are happy to have the assistance of Domestic Protection," the third, unnamed agent added. He stood behind Barry and Marsh, his face in the shadows. "After all, we are all on the same side."

Matthew looked unhappy, but he did not resist. The truth was that very few of England's magicians took Domestic Protection, or Deep as it was frequently referred to, seriously. For any crimes of a non-magical nature, the ordinary police force served their community's needs, the same as any other citizen. For crimes of national importance or international intrigue, Intelligence rooted them out and enacted justice. If a magical crime succeeded in also breaking England's laws, the Department of Magical Crimes hidden within Scotland Yard would take over. Domestic Protection was, as Agent Barry had sneered, left to handle the smallest of offenses—someone carelessly using magic where non-magical persons might see it, or casting an unpleasant-but-not-fatal curse against another magician. Grey magic, as Lennox Davies called it. Not serious enough to be evil, but not pure enough to be good.

Maia knew, through Helen, that Matthew was hoping to work with Intelligence at some point, and considered Domestic Protection a first step along that path. He likely did not want to do anything now to damage his chances later on.

"We'll take the body to the morgue, there to be examined by our best curse experts," Agent Marsh said. "Driver, will you see to it they are informed of where to go and how virulent this curse is?" The other agent nodded and slipped back out the door, presumably to go escort MI's curse experts to the morgue, wherever that was. "Our special cleansing team is now on the way to purify these premises. If you like to take witness statements, Radcliffe, I'll collect them once you've finished."

"Right," said Matthew, seeming relieved at being given something to do.

"I suggest you start with me," Maia said. "Since I was the first on the scene. Helen and Aunt Amelia came in at the same time."

Matthew opened his mouth, but Agent Barry raised his eyebrows. "Do you generally take orders from civilians, Radcliffe?" he asked in a soft voice. He flicked a quick, dismissive glance at Maia. "Perhaps this apprentice is unaware of protocol, but in MI, at least, we start at the top and work our way down."

"In any case, I was here only moments after Maia, and my butler saw it all," Aunt Amelia interrupted. "There is no need to question these young ladies at all."

Maia pinched her lips together to keep from venting her anger in front of all these people. Did Aunt Amelia think she was going to throw her career away and join Intelligence as soon as she qualified as a magician simply by talking to an agent?

It seemed she did. That was the reason she jabbed Maia so frequently for her role in that four-years'-past affair, and why she strove so urgently to keep her apart from Len. Aunt Amelia insisted Maia's magical talent was enough to make her a regional governor, or even Head Magician of the Circle, and she had no intention of letting her niece "waste" that talent on something so mundane as Intelligence, nor to let her be even tempted by it through talking with an agent.

"But that's nonsense, we were right here for the entire thing, and we might have seen something Miss Rawlings missed!" Helen burst out.

"I hardly think apprentices could have noticed something a senior magician did not," said Barry, ignoring the raised eyebrow from his partner.

Helen tossed her head. "I am a Journeyman."

"Protocol does dictate—" Agent Marsh began.

Barry turned on her with a swiftness that put Maia in mind of a striking snake. "Protocol does not get the job done, Agent Marsh," he said in a low, controlled voice. "Or have you forgotten Gizeh?"

Maia still couldn't make out the taller woman's features, but the flatness of her voice told of deep emotion carefully suppressed. "No, Barry, I've not forgotten any of it."

"But I've never been part of an official investigation before!" Helen protested.

Barry, seemingly satisfied with Agent Marsh's

capitulation, shrugged and turned back to the body. "Radcliffe, can't you even control your sister?" he tossed over his shoulder.

"You aren't helping things, Helen," Matthew hissed. He cleared his throat. "Right you are, Barry, Miss Rawlings. Ladies, this is not a fitting scene for the two of you. I am sure you are most distressed by the, er, distressing death you witnessed ..." The words died in his throat at the identical steely glares the young ladies in question were giving him. Anything less distressed could hardly be imagined. He took a deep breath and tried again. "You can best assist the investigation by going about your business as though nothing were wrong. Er, Helen, weren't you and Maia going to do some shopping today ...?"

"Mr. Radcliffe and Agent Barry are perfectly right," said Aunt Amelia with a smug expression. "As I told you girls earlier, this is no place for you. Off you go now, shoo." She flapped her hands at them as though they were chickens, only she was shooing them outside the coop instead of in. Within moments, Maia found herself with coat, hat, and gloves on, and the two were shut out—literally—from the action.

"Well," said Helen, straightening her hat and turning away from the closed front door. "I call that positively unfair."

Maia glanced down at her hands. A magician's aura—the traces left behind after working a spell or when one's magic was leaking out of control—was generally invisible to everyone but the said magician. Right now, the glimmers of silver shining through her tan kid gloves were bright enough she was surprised Helen seemed unaware of her struggle to keep the magic from bursting free of her control.

If she wasn't careful, she was going to set Aunt Amelia's

spiraea on fire right here on the front steps for all the neighbors to see.

It wasn't merely the indignity of being treated as a child—she, who had been running her family's home since she was fourteen and her sisters had driven away their first housekeeper, who had been a nurse in France during the war, who had stopped a magical conspiracy which would have destroyed England four years ago when she had barely even learned of her abilities.

It was that this Barry seemed more concerned for prestige than for doing a thorough job. It was that Agent Marsh had something chilling about her, something that unsettled Maia without her being able to articulate why. As for Matthew—well, she couldn't be too hard on Matthew, he was in rather an impossible position, though she did wish he'd shown more backbone. But Aunt Amelia ...! Did no one involved in this case care at all about the man who now lay dead? They wanted the curse contained, the culprit caught, the world back as it should be. All laudable goals, but none of the people involved seemed to care that a man had been alive and was now dead.

Maia slowly clenched and opened her hands, breathing in through her nose and out through her mouth, focusing on stuffing her magic back down within its proper bonds. It felt, as always, like wrestling a feather mattress back into its tick, and even after it was safely confined, there were a few puffs and feathers of power left floating. Nothing too dangerous, though—nothing that would explode anything or anyone.

Helen, still unaware of Maia's struggle, made her way down to the street and looked both ways. "Shall we do our shopping, then, since we aren't allowed anything more exciting?"

Maia narrowed her eyes. Ever since she was a child, being told she was not permitted to do something was the surest way to pique her interest in that very thing. "You may, if you wish," she said. "I have other plans."

Helen looked back at her and laughed. "You have something devilish in mind, I can tell," she said. "Whatever it is, count me in."

A light entered Maia's hazel blue eyes. She had spent too many years weighted down with the responsibility of her careless and highly dramatic family, believing she was too dull and staid to ever have an interesting life. Ever since discovering her magic and coming to London to train with Aunt Amelia, she had delighted in proving herself wrong.

"I merely thought I might chat with some of the neighbors, see if any of them saw or heard anything interesting," Maia said. "That can't be considered interfering— we are merely gossiping and being neighborly, correct?"

"Just as young women ought to do," Helen said, fluttering her long eyelashes. She eyed Maia's clothing. "It is unfortunate that you are wearing that," she said. "You don't look at all appropriate for chatting with the neighbors in that ancient skirt and those shoes. I'd glamour you something different—" glamours were Helen's speciality— "But non-magical eyes can't see glamours, so it would be wasted effort."

Maia barely listened to this. She had gotten into the habit of tuning Helen out whenever she dragged glamours into the conversation. They might be fascinating to the other girl, but they held little interest for her. "Never mind, old thing," she said vaguely. "There's not much point in talking to the owners of the nearby houses, anyway. Most of them wouldn't notice an interesting occurrence if it leapt up and bit them on the nose." Rather like Aunt Amelia. "The servants, however, always know everything. And they won't care if I am less than impeccably dressed."

Helen laughed again and sighed. "Oh dear, you really don't know anything at all about servants, do you?"

"I was on very good relations with all our servants at Stanbury, thank you very much," Maia said. The ones Mother, Ellie and Merry didn't scare off, that was.

Helen waved a hand. "Oh, country servants, old retainers, families who all know each other and all that. Of course they wouldn't care how you were dressed. I'm sure you were 'the eldest Whitney daughter' no matter where you went within the village and shopkeepers always tipped their hat to you and saved you the best cuts of meat without you even asking."

"I ..." Maia couldn't deny any of it.

"But London servants, my dear! If they think you are dressing beneath your station, they won't give you the time of day."

It was Maia's turn to sigh. Helen was London born and bred and kept her finger unerringly on the social pulse of the city. There was nothing for it.

"*Abscondo meum in manifestis conspectu.*" She had never revealed to anyone else that she knew this spell. It was one of Len's favorites, and she'd learned it from him, which alone was a good reason to keep it secret from Aunt Amelia. It did not turn her invisible, but allowed her to blend in with her surroundings. Len called it his chameleon spell, and Maia found it quite useful.

Helen stared, and blinked. She reached out a tentative finger and poked at Maia's arm, looking relieved to make contact. "I say," she said in a hushed voice. "Do teach me that!

It would be splendid for sneaking out of the house without Mother knowing."

Maia ignored this. "Wait for me at the corner," she said. "I'll sneak in the back door, run upstairs and change, and then join you."

"Wear that navy suit with the silver embroidery," Helen ordered. "And heels!"

Maia loathed heels—she was tall enough as it was, though shorter than Agent Marsh, and heels made her wobble when she walked—but if she thought of it as a disguise, something Sherlock Holmes would put on in order to hunt down clues, she could just about bear them.

**

None of the servants to either side of Aunt Amelia's had heard or seen anything, or at least would not admit it to Maia and Helen. Maia found herself wishing for Len's manservant Becket. He was shy but kind-hearted, and servants would be far more likely to talk freely to him than to ladies of gentility. No matter! She had heard nothing from Len to indicate he was off on another mission, so she assumed they would meet for their monthly tea tomorrow as planned. If she and Helen had no luck here, she would ask to borrow Becket and see if he came up with more results.

However, the house across the street yielded her something. The scullery maid, a girl with flaming red hair that made Maia's look positively muddy, had stepped outside "for a spot of fresh air," she said, though from her breath Maia suspected she'd gone out to smoke a cigarette, and had seen the entire thing through the railings.

"Saw 'im plain as day, I did," said the girl, who went by the improbable name of Angelina. "Swaggered right up to the front door all prim an' proper, pressed the doorbell, and then 'e froze, like that," snapping her finger, "an' when the door opened, 'e just keeled over inside. 'Gent's got a stomach pain,' I said to meself, but then Cook called me back inside and I didn't see no more. Is 'e dead then, miss?"

"Yes, I'm afraid so," Maia said. "The, ah, undertaker is taking him away now." She and Angelina watched as Barry and three other men brought out the tightly-wrapped body on a stretcher.

"Poor chap. Were 'e a friend of the family?"

"Distant relative," Maia improvised wildly. "Very distant. Thank you for your time." She pressed a coin into Angelina's hand and hurried away to where Helen was frantically motioning to her from the street.

"We'll be seen!" she hissed. "Matthew is coming now. Do that, that not-visible spell you did earlier, quick!"

"Very well, but you'll have to hold quite still," Maia said, swallowing her nerves. She'd never done this to cover anyone but herself before. She closed her eyes and sketched a quick shape in the air with her forefinger, something that, if drawn by pencil, might have looked like a child's rendering of a lizard. Hand motions were not necessary, but they did help focus one's concentration. Aunt Amelia despised such concessions, naturally, but for this, Maia thought she needed all the help she could get.

"*Abscondo meum in manifestis conspectu*," she whispered, and felt the spell tug and take hold. Out of the corner of her eye, she saw that Helen was slowly fading from sight. Maia released her breath. It had worked!

Matthew and the lesser agents assigned to him scattered

and converged upon the neighboring houses, no doubt in search of the same information Maia and Helen had just scrounged. At least he was bothering with that, even if he wouldn't interview her and Helen! As soon as their attention was engaged, Maia let the spell slowly dissipate as she and Helen backed away and slipped around the corner. Judging they were safe enough now, Maia relayed Angelina's story to Helen.

The shorter girl nodded. "That's what the housemaid of the place next to that one said, too. I think she and your Angelina were out smoking together, actually." Helen waved a hand in front of her face. Nobody was entirely certain why, but nicotine and magic did not react well to each other, and most magicians avoided cigarette smoke as much as possible.

"She said the mystery man walked to your aunt's house, brisk and fit as a flea, rang the bell, and then doubled over as if he had a stomach pain and reeled inside once the door opened. The maid didn't see anyone else anywhere near until I came by a few minutes later."

Maia nibbled her lower lip as she thought. "Do you suppose it could have been someone so familiar they wouldn't even have noticed him? A delivery man, or the post?"

Helen shook her head, grinning. "I read detective novels too, I'll have you know! I asked the maid that, and she insisted. It's the wrong time for the post, nobody delivers on Fridays, no chimney sweeps or window cleaners around, nothing. Only birds and our dead man."

Maia tossed her hands in the air. "It doesn't make sense! That spell couldn't have been on him long. With the amount of residue leaking off it by the time Aunt examined the body, he must have collapsed the instant it was cast. The assailant must have been in hiding, that's the only explanation."

"Not many places to hide on a London residential street," Helen pointed out. "Unless he was in the area," indicating the sunken servants' entrance, "but then the maids would have seen him. Around the corner?"

Maia stopped and turned. She looked up and down the street, then shook her head. "Maybe. But you can't see Aunt Amelia's house from here. I admit, I don't know enough about curses, perhaps the victim could have walked that far— but no, that doesn't work, either, because the maids saw him walk up and he was fine. Maybe it was a chameleon spell."

"Perhaps. But what do we do now? If we'd had more time, we might have been able to cast a discovery spell to see what recent magic had been performed in the area, but Matthew and his people will surely do that themselves, as well as finish interviewing everyone on the street. It seems as though we've only a few options open to us," Helen continued. "We can try to hunt down the victim's identity, but I admit frankly I've no idea how to do that. We can try to research the spell that was cast on him, but I don't exactly know how to investigate curses without setting off quite a number of people's alarms, including my mother. Or," she finished, brightening. "We can go shopping as we were told to do, and rack our brains for ideas at the same time as we find smashing frocks for the Ball."

Maia didn't like it, but she had to admit Helen had a point.

✳

If you enjoyed this sneak peek, keep an eye out for
<u>*Glamours and Gunshots*</u>*, coming soon!*

www.ingramcontent.com/pod-product-compliance
Lightning Source LLC
Chambersburg PA
CBHW030538130626
46552CB00006B/2315